"I'm not looking **especially with so** **with,"** Henrik said

Jo looked confused. "
was thinking when I asked where you've been."

"Usually that's why women ask. I'm not looking for anything long-term, which I mentioned the night we met."

Her eyes narrowed. "And I believe I said the same thing to you. I'm only here for a year, Henrik. And I've already had my great love."

"Yes, I feel the same," he said softly.

"Right." There was sympathy in her gaze. "I was just getting to know you, and…" She trailed off nervously. "There's no easy way to tell you this, Henrik, and honestly, if you were a stranger passing through, this would be a moot point anyway. But since you're from here and we'll be seeing each other around…"

"You're rambling."

"I know." She folded her hands in her lap. "I'm pregnant, Henrik. And the baby's yours."

Dear Reader,

Thank you for picking up a copy of Josephine and Henrik's story, *Paramedic's One-Night Baby Bombshell*.

Newfoundland has always been somewhere I've wanted to visit. I had a fun time writing this book set on Fogo Island and researching sea cucumbers, which is something I never thought I would ever do!

Josephine is a widow and looking to feel again. An escape away from Toronto for a year to a slower pace of life seems like the perfect way to find herself again.

Henrik's been so hurt in the past, he just can't seem to open his heart and certainly has no interest in finding a happily-ever-after. That is, until his one-night stand with the new doctor in town.

I hope you enjoy Josephine and Henrik's story.

I love hearing from readers, so please drop by my website, www.amyruttan.com.

With warmest wishes,

Amy Ruttan

PARAMEDIC'S ONE-NIGHT BABY BOMBSHELL

———

AMY RUTTAN

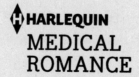

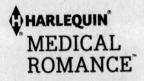

HARLEQUIN®
MEDICAL
ROMANCE™

Recycling programs
for this product may
not exist in your area.

ISBN-13: 978-1-335-73755-7

Paramedic's One-Night Baby Bombshell

Copyright © 2022 by Amy Ruttan

Harlequin Enterprises ULC
22 Adelaide St. West, 41st Floor
Toronto, Ontario M5H 4E3, Canada
www.Harlequin.com

Printed in U.S.A.

Born and raised just outside Toronto, Ontario, **Amy Ruttan** fled the big city to settle down with the country boy of her dreams. After the birth of her second child, Amy was lucky enough to realize her lifelong dream of becoming a romance author. When she's not furiously typing away at her computer, she's mom to three wonderful children, who use her as a personal taxi and chef.

Books by Amy Ruttan

Harlequin Medical Romance

Portland Midwives

The Doctor She Should Resist

Caribbean Island Hospital

Reunited with Her Surgeon Boss
A Ring for His Pregnant Midwife

First Response

Pregnant with the Paramedic's Baby

Baby Bombshell for the Doctor Prince
Reunited with Her Hot-Shot Surgeon
A Reunion, a Wedding, a Family
Twin Surprise for the Baby Doctor
Falling for the Billionaire Doc
Falling for His Runaway Nurse

Visit the Author Profile page
at Harlequin.com for more titles.

For my aunt Margaret. You were a true lover of all books. You were a great storyteller and I'll miss you tremendously. Fly free.

CHAPTER ONE

Fogo Island, Newfoundland

WHAT AM I doing here?

Dr. Josephine York—Jo—looked around the dark little pub that was filled with locals of Nubbin's Harbor, which was going to be her new home for the next year.

It seemed friendly enough. It just wasn't her scene. If there were pubs like this in Toronto, it wasn't her usual place to go.

Not that she went anywhere.

You're here now. This is the first step out of your comfort zone.

If there was going to be any kind of change in her life, then she had to do things out of the ordinary. She had to rip the bandage off and live again. She'd been living in grief and loneliness for far too long.

This was an adventure.

Or at least, that's what she kept telling herself.

This little inn was not her first choice. She'd rather stay in the new hotel, which wasn't far from here, but they had been full up since the prime season for icebergs was coming. It would mean, according to the owner of the place she was staying at, that Nubbin's Harbor and indeed all of Fogo would be full of tourists from all over the world.

People came to watch the big hunks of ice make their way south from the Arctic.

Jo had seen pictures and was looking forward to seeing it firsthand.

Still, it meant lodgings were sparse so she should be thankful for what she'd got, even if she was a bit anxious at the moment.

At least the little hotel above a pub had rave reviews. It was a good-enough place to stay until her apartment became available in a couple of weeks. Gary was lending her his place, and until he left, the hotel would have to be her home. At least she'd had the sense to think ahead, when Gary had asked her to take over his practice, to buying a small car here online so it was ready for her when she'd landed in the capital city, St. John's.

She needed a vehicle to get around Newfoundland with ease.

Not that she'd seen much of the island driving four hours through the rain and then taking an hour-long ferry ride to get to the island and then another hour to wind her way up toward Nubbin's Harbor where Gary's practice was located.

It was bitterly cold for a spring day this late in April, but then the weather had been nasty all day since she'd left St. John's, and headed northeast toward Fogo Island, which was an island off another island. Yesterday, when she'd landed in St. John's after her flight from Toronto, she had felt such hope.

The sun was shining.

It was a beautiful spring day.

It was mild, the Atlantic was blue. And on that sunny first day in the capital, the brightly colored houses and the blue sky had given Jo hope that she'd made the right decision to change her life completely and move to the eastern coast of Canada, leaving everything she knew behind.

It had put Jo in such an optimistic mood. It made her think, for a nanosecond, that leaving her life in Toronto was definitely the right thing to do. That even at thirty-eight, with a settled surgical practice, a house, and a great salary in the best city in the world, she wasn't too old for an adventure or for an abrupt change.

There had been a time in her life when she'd been more carefree. Once.

As she glanced around the small pub on the edge of what people thought was one of the four corners of a flat earth, she suddenly wasn't so sure about her decisions.

Come on, Jo. Where is your sense of adventure?

And she smiled to herself thinking of her late husband's voice. Usually she tried not to think about him at all. She would throw herself into her work instead, so she could ignore the pain.

Only, right now, she was glad to remember his voice. David had always wanted to live life to the fullest. He'd been an adventure seeker to the max.

He was such an avid adventurer that he'd even had to depart this mortal coil well before she did.

A lump formed in her throat as that sweet memory faded to pain, like it always did. It wasn't as sharp as it had been, but it was still there, nonetheless. Gnawing at her and relentless at times.

He'd been gone for three years.

And it hadn't been his choice to leave her.

An aneurysm had decided that course of their life.

Don't think about it.

David had been dead for three years, and she needed to live again.

She wanted to feel again, she told herself.

Experience life.

She'd always love him. Losing him would always hurt, but this was a fresh start, and she needed to grasp it with both hands.

She straightened her spine and got up, alone in a pub full of locals.

What she needed right now was a drink.

Jo made her way to the bar and sat down on an empty stool at the far end. She was completely out of place in a room of flannel-clad, bearded men.

The live music from the house band didn't help her clear her head.

And as she sat there, she was trying to remember why she had agreed to this change.

Because David completely haunts your life in

Toronto, and you need to move on, a small voice reminded her.

It was true.

David was everywhere back home.

Even at work in the hospital. That's where she'd met him, where they'd worked together and where he'd ended up after she'd frantically called an ambulance finding him unresponsive one morning.

She had come to the farthest corner of Canada, and yet, he was still here. Still around her. His memory was still reminding her of all the hopes and dreams they had planned.

A family.

Happiness.

Adventure and love.

Dreams that were long gone now.

Except, she needed a change. An escape. She wanted to feel alive again, even though that prospect was scary indeed.

So a change of scenery was just what the doctor ordered. Another province, the other side of the country, was as different as she'd dared to go at the moment.

David would've totally been up for an adventure like this, and this time so was she.

Jo was nervous, but she needed to get out of this rut she had been stuck in.

Maybe she could rediscover the woman who'd loved life.

"What'll you be having, miss?" the barkeep

asked, smiling and his eyes twinkling behind his bushy eyebrows.

"Some white wine?" she said.

He nodded. "Coming right up."

Jo relaxed a little and took a glance around the pub. It might've seemed dark and kind of off-putting at first, but as she had a glance around it, she relaxed. It was actually pretty homey, and the more she looked at the patrons, the more she realized that they seemed genuinely happy.

It had to be the weather that was off-putting.

That was it. And miserable weather couldn't last forever. At least, she hoped it couldn't.

Her friend Gary loved his life on Fogo, and the only reason he was leaving his work here was because he'd been offered the amazing chance to teach at a prestigious medical school in Munich. Gary hadn't wanted to leave his practice to just anyone, and so he'd reached out to her.

She and Gary had met in college. They'd gone to medical school together and become fast friends.

"Take over my practice, Jo," Gary had said.

"Are you sure it's right for me?"

"I trust you with my patients, and you need a change," Gary had urged gently.

"Do I?"

"Yes. Ever since David died...you sound lost. Hollow."

"I am," she'd whispered, finally admitting it to someone.

"You were such a free spirit. It's what I always loved about you. It's what David loved about you," Gary had said. "You have to learn to live again."

"I'm not sure."

"You want to, though. I know it, and David would want you to as well."

"I do," she'd said, because Gary was right.

"Come to Fogo then. See what I've been raving about. Please say you'll take care of my place?"

Gary had convinced her. He wasn't wrong. So Jo had jumped at the chance to escape her ghosts in Toronto and try to figure out how to live again. She'd been merely existing in a fog for far too long.

She laughed to herself as she thought about that.

Since she'd arrived here she hadn't seen a hair of the place because it had been mostly covered by a fog bank from the rain. Hopefully it would clear up.

"Here you go, miss." The barkeeper slid the glass of wine toward her. "Niagara's finest!"

"You don't have a local wine?" she asked.

"You won't be wanting the local wine," a voice said at the end of the bar.

She glanced over, and her breath caught in her throat at the tall, hunched-over, not-so-scruffy-looking young Viking a few seats down. He had the most brilliant blue eyes that she'd ever seen, under a dark mop of hair.

When his gaze locked on hers, a jolt of familiarity coursed through her, which made her blood heat. It was as though the instant she met his intense regard, it felt like he was a kindred spirit.

Like he could see right through to her inner pain.

Like he knew her.

It had been like that when she'd met David.

Her pulse began to race, and she could feel a blush creeping up her neck to her cheeks. She averted her eyes, trying to calm her nerves, but her gaze immediately tracked back to the large tattoo that started at the base of his left wrist and wound its way up his muscular forearm and disappeared under the sleeve of his fitted cotton T-shirt. That shirt didn't hide any of his well-defined muscles, and a coil of heat unfurled in her belly.

It had been a long time since she'd felt this heat, this kind of attraction for another man.

It was good to feel that jolt of desire again.

There was a half smile just underneath his well-kept beard.

He was nursing a pint of beer, and she couldn't help but smile back at him.

"There be nothing wrong with Nubbin's Harbor wine," the barman said brusquely. "It's just only local folk can handle it."

"Aw, Lloyd, you know that's not it at all," the handsome man said. "It's disgusting, that's why."

Lloyd puffed his chest up. "I save the Niagara stuff for the toffs from Ontario."

Jo smiled. "How did you know I was from Ontario?"

"Your accent is a dead giveaway," Lloyd stated, moving away, and she couldn't help but laugh under her breath. She never really thought of herself as having an accent before, but since she'd landed in the Maritimes and in Newfoundland, she was the one with the accent now.

"Don't mind Lloyd. He's very passionate about anything to do with Fogo Island," the handsome stranger said.

"I can't say that I blame him. It's good to be so fervent about your home."

The Viking nodded. "Aye, and we do have some good things here you should try."

"I wouldn't mind trying some local things. Although, I wouldn't have pegged Fogo Island as a hot spot for a winery. I thought it needed to be a bit warmer and have a bit more soil over the rock?"

The stranger smiled, those blue eyes twinkling, making her swoon again. "Aye, it's a pretty sad sort of wine that Lloyd brews himself. He has a few grape vines in a pathetic ramshackle of a greenhouse, and he fancies himself a vintner. If you're not used to strong stuff or alcohol that tastes like turpentine, I would steer clear of it. And screech too."

"Screech?" she asked, curious.

"Come on, every Canadian knows about screech."

"I guess I've been living under a rock, then. I've never heard of it."

The stranger slid a barstool closer, his eyebrow cocking. "You've seriously never heard of screech?"

"No. Is it like moonshine?" she asked.

His eyes widened, and then he smiled. "No, but maybe it has a similar kick. It's rum—untempered rum. It's from the days we would trade salted fish to Jamaica in exchange for rum. Those who first started drinking it didn't mind its potency."

"I don't mind rum."

There was a mischievous look in his eyes. "I'm thinking that you would be minding this."

Jo had never been one to back down from a challenge, and if she was going to fit in here, she might as well get used to some of the local flair. Not that she was sure that *flair* was the right word, but *untempered rum* sounded a bit reckless, even though in her college days she could drink anyone she wanted to under the table.

At least she wasn't on duty yet.

Maybe tonight was the night she became an honorary screecher.

"I think I can handle it, but first… I'd like to know your name. I don't usually drink with strangers in an unfamiliar bar."

He held out his hand. "Henrik."

She took his large, strong hand in hers.

The simple touch sent a ripple of electric heat through her, a rush of endorphins that were most welcome.

And in that one instant she pictured what it would be like to have those hands on her body.

Touching her.

Waking her up from her fog.

"My name is Josephine." Strangers got the long version of her name. Only those close to her called her Jo.

Henrik turned to the barkeep. "Lloyd, our friend from Toronto wants to try a fine glass of screech!"

The music stopped, and Jo's eyes widened as a bunch of people in the pub turned around in their seats to eye her in fascination and amusement.

Lloyd was grinning as he pulled out a bottle and poured her a glass. "This is the finest I have, miss."

Usually she corrected the person and told them her title was *Doctor*, but tonight she just wanted to be a stranger.

To observe.

The townsfolk would learn soon enough who she was. She didn't want questions tonight. Especially since all eyes were on her, and she was about to guzzle down a shot of untempered rum.

Jo held the shot glass up.

"Wait!" someone shouted. "If she be from the mainland, then she needs to be screeched in."

Henrik was chuckling, and Jo was now getting a bit nervous.

"Pardon?" she asked, clearing her throat. "I need to be what?"

"You need to be screeched in, lass," Lloyd stated. "Does anyone have a cod?"

There were a lot of loud voices and some discussion, and Jo felt bewildered as she looked at Henrik. "Cod?"

He nodded. "You have to kiss a cod and swear an oath. If you're not from here, then it's the rules. I was trying to spare you, but since Lloyd's already announced it, I think you're kind of stuck."

"You can't be serious about kissing a fish?" Jo asked, laughing nervously as she watched Lloyd digging around in a freezer.

Henrik shrugged. "It's tradition."

"Aha! She ain't fresh, but she'll do!" Lloyd held up a massive frozen bug-eyed whole cod, much to the entertainment of the patrons.

A knot was forming in the pit of Jo's stomach. A shot of alcohol was not worth this.

Henrik, as if sensing her trepidation leaned over and whispered in her ear. "You can't back out now. Would be an insult to do so."

You wanted to fit in, Josephine. This is how you do it.

The last thing she wanted to do was insult potential patients.

It wouldn't hurt to kiss a freaking cod.

Some ceremonious fiddle music was being played in the background as the fish was brought over to the bar.

"She needs to kiss the fish and recite the credo!" someone called out.

Jo was staring at the frozen face, mouth agape, of the ugliest fish she had ever seen. "Seriously?"

Henrik nodded. "There's the piece of paper, with the credo written on it. Go on. Recite it, kiss the fish and down the screech."

Joe took a deep breath, picked up the piece of paper and read from it. "*From the waters of the Avalon to the shores of Labrador, We've always stuck together, with a rant and with a roar. To those who've never been, soon they'll understand, From coast to coast, we raise a toast. We love thee, Newfoundland!*"

There was a loud cheer.

"Now, pucker up," Henrik teased.

Joe glared at him. Gripped the bar with her two hands, closed her eyes and kissed the cold fish on the lips. It was so gross that she instantly grabbed the rum to douse the taste of cod and downed it.

It was rough.

It burned.

It was the worst-tasting, strongest thing she had ever had.

There was a lot more cheering, but she began to cough and held onto the edge of the bar for dear life as that liquor burned a path through her esophageal tract.

"Josephine, are you okay?" Henrik asked, while

some of the others in the bar took their turns kissing the fish and dancing.

"I think the local wine might've been better," she managed to get out.

Henrik laughed. "Come on, let's get some air."

Jo gladly went with Henrik. She instinctively knew he was someone she could trust, and she liked how he made her feel. She wanted to get to know him better, even if only for one night, because she wasn't ready for any kind of relationship. She also needed to get away from that cod. She hadn't kissed anyone since her husband had passed. It figured: the first time she managed to get up the courage to be intimate with anyone and it was a dead fish.

Henrik didn't think that the beautiful stranger had it in her.

Usually, when he came across tourists that were alone and female, they weren't really into having a screech-in. Those that participated in the ceremony were usually with a group of friends and were already three sheets to the wind. They would also approach him. Not that anything would ever happen the first night. When he took them to his bed, they were always sober.

Of course, most tourists knew what screech was and didn't have to ask. Although something nagged at him that she wasn't a usual tourist, only because she was on her own. She seemed out of place.

A little lost. He knew that look well. He'd seen it reflected in his own eyes from time to time.

He admired her strength and her determination to take on the challenge, sober.

Henrik didn't often find those qualities in the women that passed through Fogo Island, and they were his specialty. Women who just passed through. Those were his preference because then it was never long-term.

It was always short-term.

It was a fling.

There was no commitment, and that was exactly what Henrik Nielsen wanted.

He had tried to have forever, and that had bitten him squarely on his nose, and he wasn't falling for that again. So he had vacation flings with the women he fancied, and that was all. It was perfect.

Not that he had been planning on meeting anyone tonight.

He usually liked to stick around for a while. At least a week. That's how long women tended to stay, but he couldn't this time. He was headed out of town for a month with the coast guard for training at sea rescue farther up the coast of Labrador.

And he was flying out tomorrow morning. Even by his standards, that wasn't enough time for a fling. He should walk away from her, but he'd discovered he couldn't.

There had been something in her eyes. Almost like he saw himself reflected back in them, and he was incredibly drawn to her. He couldn't quite pin it down, but he just wasn't able to tear himself away. Maybe because she was quiet and reserved, yet spoke her mind, and she seemed to be kind and gentle.

Most women were only with him for one thing, and he was fine with that.

He didn't want a relationship.

Liar.

He shook that voice away.

All he'd planned tonight was a quiet pint at Lloyd's before he shipped out, and then she'd walked into the pub.

Josephine had absolutely taken his breath away.

It was like he had been hit by a bolt of lightning the moment their eyes met across the bar.

She was stunning. And he couldn't remember the last time he'd seen a woman who had taken his breath away like that.

Yes, you can. Melissa.

It had been some time since he'd really let himself think about the woman who had broken his heart. He had been so in love with Melissa. They had grown up together here in Nubbin's Harbor. She'd moved away to Vancouver, but then when she and Henrik were both twenty-two, she'd come back to stay with her grandparents for a bit. He'd fallen head over heels for her.

She had family all over Fogo, and they were Newfoundlanders through and through.

Just like his family.

For him, it was only natural they should get married. They were going to run away together because her family didn't want them to get married right away, and neither did his late grandmother, who'd raised him when his parents had died.

She'd wanted him to make a life for himself first, but he was a fool and had been blinded by love.

Maybe they knew more than he did, because he had been so smitten he couldn't see. He wanted the same kind of love his late parents had had when they'd been alive and it had been the three of them against the world, until that storm had struck, leaving him orphaned.

Henrik had never forgotten the love, though. The feeling of family. He'd wanted that so badly, and he thought he'd found it with Melissa.

Only, he hadn't.

He'd started his paramedic training, then come back for her so they could marry, but she was already gone. She'd moved back to the West Coast. She'd decided she didn't want to stay on Fogo, and he couldn't leave his gran or his life in Newfoundland.

All that Melissa had left for him was a note saying goodbye.

He'd been heartbroken, embarrassed, humiliated. Love was only an illusion. Melissa had shattered his trust, and Henrik had dealt with enough pain. It was far easier to harden his heart.

As much as he longed for family, he knew the anguish of losing it all and being left alone.

That was something he never wanted to feel again.

So he'd focused on his career as a first responder. That was what he'd always wanted to do. Save lives so others didn't feel pain or loss like he had. He'd worked long days and nights. Work kept him so busy that he didn't think about how badly Melissa had hurt him.

Much.

All he could rely on was Fogo Island and his work.

Those two things never let him down like love had.

Sweeping beautiful strangers off their feet for a week was a distraction. It was safe because he liked being a vacation boyfriend. He knew better than to fall deeply for a woman not from the Rock. Or to ever fall in love. The island didn't change, but people left.

He certainly wasn't ever going to leave.

All his precious memories were here. Fogo was in his blood… It was his roots.

It was home.

If he left, he'd let down the memories of his ancestors.

And since he was the only one who remained, he had to stay so he'd never forget. And so Fogo would never forget his family.

Flings were a nice distraction from loneliness. It was easy, there were no strings and, because he was planning on leaving tomorrow, he hadn't thought of approaching Josephine, the woman with the honey-colored hair and beautiful green eyes who sat a couple seats down at the bar.

Yet, he couldn't help himself. Something about her drew him to her.

And when she'd leaned over, those luscious pink lips puckering up to kiss the cod, for the first time in his almost thirty-one years, he'd envied a fish.

"How was it?" he asked, as they headed outside.

She reached out and gripped his arm as if holding on for dear life. "God-awful."

He laughed. "Aye, well, it is strong."

"No, I wasn't commenting on the screech, though it does have a very antiseptic burn to it."

"Then, what?"

"The cod." Josephine shuddered. "That is a… gross tradition."

Henrik chuckled softly. "Some people like to eat the lips of the cod and the cheeks."

"Are you serious?"

"Have I lied to you yet?" he teased, laughing.

"I would never call you a liar," she said.

"I know, but cod lips and cheeks are quite the delicacy."

"That sounds terrifying." Shivering, she pulled her wrap tighter around her.

Henrik pulled off his sherpa jacket and wrapped it around her.

"Thanks," she whispered, through chattering teeth.

"My pleasure. Anyone who drinks screech like that and complains about the cod more than the liquor deserves my respect and admiration."

She laughed, and then he smiled. Josephine had a wonderful laugh that warmed his heart. It was a good thing that he was leaving tomorrow. She would be a dangerous woman to get to know: he was feeling things toward her that he'd sworn he would never allow again.

"I should try and find some dinner or something. I haven't eaten a thing since I left St. John's this morning."

"Well, Cherry's Kitchen is just around the corner. She has the best home-cooked food around."

"That sounds good."

She seemed to hesitate, her cheeks flushing pink. "I don't usually do this, but I'm alone, and you seem nice…and you know Fogo."

"Aye, I am, and I do." He grinned, winking.

"Would you like to join me? I could use some company."

Say no. Say no.

"I'd like that." He cursed himself inwardly at not being able to resist her.

He should go home and get some sleep, only he couldn't seem to make himself leave.

Why was he so drawn to her? When they had shaken hands, he'd felt a rush of fire in his veins. A tingle of anticipation as he'd pictured how soft and warm the rest of her was.

Henrik swallowed, his mouth dry and his pulse thundering in his ears.

What harm could one night do?

It might be a pleasant way to pass the time before he left. They made their way around the corner to Cherry's Kitchen.

It was quiet, and they found a table near the back. Josephine took off his coat and handed it back to him as they sat down. He wanted to ask her why she was passing through. He wanted to get to know her better, which was strange. He never did want to know much about a woman he was seeing for such a short time.

And that was maybe because he wasn't planning on doing anything with her.

What was coming over him?

You're lonely.

But he shook that thought away. Loneliness was easier to bear than pain.

Was it, though?

"What's good here?" Josephine asked, interrupting his thoughts.

"Fish?" he teased.

Josephine wrinkled her nose. "I think I'll stick to the salad tonight."

"Because of the fish?" he asked, trying not to smile.

"Are you telling me the salad isn't safe to eat? Is there fish in the salad?"

Henrik laughed and winked. "You're safe. I'm just having a bit of fun with you."

"That's a relief."

Henrik leaned over the table. "You're not going to fare very well here if you dislike fish."

"I don't hate fish… It's just I'm going to have nightmares of fish lips for some time."

"Who wouldn't?" Henrik agreed.

The waitress came over and took their orders and assured Josephine that there was no fish in the beet salad.

"So tell me about Fogo," Josephine said.

"What would you like to know?" he asked.

"If there's anything in particular I should see while I'm here?"

"The Fogo Island Inn is a marvel, and there's lots of little shops, craft stores to visit. You should really buy a Fogo Island quilt. They keep you warm in the winter."

"You're very versed in crafts," she teased.

Henrik grinned. "Well, I am a man of mystery."

Her eyes twinkled, and she tucked back her long hair. He wondered what it would feel like to run his fingers through it. It was probably soft and smelled good.

He wondered where he could kiss her that would

make her sigh. Maybe it was her neck that would do it?

"You have quite the tattoo," Josephine remarked.

Henrik glanced down. "It's a tree. My family tree and the sea. It's a part of us all, here."

She reached out and touched it. "It's very beautiful."

Her touch sent heat rushing through him.

"Thank you. Do you have any tattoos?"

"No," she said, her cheeks flushing. "I was never that brave."

"Oh? Is it the needles?"

"Yes. And pain…for myself."

He cocked a teasing eyebrow. "Oh? So you enjoy inflicting pain on others, then? I didn't think you were into that, but I'm game if you are." He'd forgotten himself for a moment. It was so easy to tease her, joke around, and he held his breath hoping he hadn't offended her.

She was smiling, but her blush deepened. "I'm not into that, but it's good to know where you're at."

She was teasing him right back.

Henrik laughed. She was wonderful to talk to. It felt like he didn't have to try so hard with her, as though he'd known her for a long time. It was like talking to one of his old friends.

It was refreshing. He hadn't felt this way in a very long time.

He wanted to get to know her better, but what was the point? He was leaving.

And so was she.

So he didn't ask. Even though he wanted to.

That thought scared him, but not enough to make him leave.

He couldn't.

She was engaging company, and he was hungrier for it than he'd realized.

The waitress brought over their food, and they had a pleasant dinner talking about nothing important, but it still felt nice.

It felt right.

Which was a scary prospect indeed. He wouldn't risk his heart for anything.

The more he talked to her, the more he forgot about all the rules that he'd put into place to keep women like her at bay. He usually compartmentalized his flings. He knew where to put them in his heart so he didn't get attached and it was easy to walk away.

Henrik was not doing that here.

Usually, that was a warning to stay away. He had been burned by love before, but since he wouldn't see her again, it might be worth the risk. He was incredibly attracted to Josephine. She was funny, smart, beautiful.

He wanted to know more about her, which made her dangerous, but his flight out tomorrow meant that it might be okay to live a bit dangerously. Even just for a night.

They paid for their meals and left Cherry's Kitchen as she was closing for the night. They walked down the hill, back to the pub and the only hotel in Nubbin's Harbor. There were a few of the locals hanging about, and there was boisterous fiddle music coming from the pub at the bottom.

"Thanks for walking me back."

"It's not a problem."

"I hope I'm not keeping you from something. Are you local?"

"Yes, but I'm leaving the island tomorrow for work."

A brief look of disappointment crossed her face. It was just a fraction of a moment, and he wasn't completely sure that it was disappointment. Maybe that's what he was feeling and he was projecting it onto her. Josephine was a stranger, after all.

A gorgeous stranger.

"You're not from here, though," Henrik teased, trying to defuse the tension that had settled between them as they stood toe to toe in the cool spring night.

"As we discussed in the bar, I'm the toff from Toronto."

"In Ontario."

"Yes, I was born and raised in Ontario's prettiest town."

"Isn't that Toronto?" he teased. "The way Torontonians talk..."

Josephine laughed. "No. Toronto is great, but it's not the prettiest town in the province."

"Oh?" he asked. "Where is that, then?"

"Goderich. It's on the southeast shore of Lake Huron."

"And what's it known for, besides being the prettiest?" he asked.

"Salt."

He raised his eyebrows. "Really?"

"What's Nubbin's Harbor known for, besides screech, Lloyd's turpentine wine and cod lips?"

He chuckled. "There's a lighthouse."

"That's it?"

"The icebergs will come soon, but the fishing that Nubbin's Harbor was known for is gone. Government restrictions and the like."

Josephine nodded. "I'm sorry."

"Most go to town to work," he sighed. "Not many have stayed."

They stood there in silence, and it began to rain.

"I better go upstairs."

"Aye, well…" He couldn't finish was he was going to say. Instead he just leaned over and kissed her on the cheek. Her skin was soft, and she smelled sweet, like vanilla. He bet those lips were just as sweet to taste. Henrik stroked her cheek with the back of his knuckles and felt her tremble. He was going to step away, but instead she grabbed him by the lapels and pulled him close.

Pulled him up against her lithe body, and he got to taste those full, soft lips that were so inviting. She deepened the kiss, her tongue entwining with his, and he cupped her silky hair in his hands as he drank her in.

It would be a bad idea, if he wasn't leaving. He was enjoying his brief time with her far too much. He wouldn't mind being hers for a week, but that's all he could give her.

Josephine was a temptation. A complete and utter temptation, and even though he should walk away, he couldn't help himself.

Especially not when she had been the one to pull him close.

She broke off the kiss. "Would you like to come up to my room for another shot of screech?"

Say no.

"Aye. I would like that."

Josephine smiled, her green eyes bewitching as she took him by the hand and led him inside the pub.

He knew he shouldn't, but the appeal was too great.

Josephine was going to be hard to walk away from, but he was certain one night wasn't going to put his heart in danger.

One night wouldn't change anything.

It never did, and Josephine would be gone when he got back.

No one ever stayed.

Only him.

* * *

Jo still couldn't quite believe this was happening. The first time she'd met David, she had been a bit rash. She had initiated their first kiss then too. David always teased her that she knew exactly what she wanted, and she'd go for it.

The moment she saw Henrik in the pub, she knew she wanted him.

She was incredibly attracted to him.

While she was with him, she felt like her old self.

And the more she talked to Henrik, the more comfortable she was.

The more she wanted him.

What she wanted was to get out of this funk. She wanted to the rip that bandage off.

Coming to Fogo for the year was to wake her up out of this haze she'd been living in the last three years. How could she move on in her life if she never took another chance? Henrik was going to be leaving soon. He was handsome and kind. She was attracted to him. He'd already mentioned he wasn't into long-term relationships, and she'd told him she wasn't either. So why not indulge?

It had been a long time since she'd felt any kind of pull like that toward another person. This was her new start. A way to find herself again. So she invited Henrik up for a drink. Truth be told, she was a bit lonely.

And scared.

It had been so wonderful to have a conversation

with a man again. After David died, she'd thrown herself into her work. It was work, and then home. That was it.

Now she needed a reset to her life.

She was trembling as she pulled out her key card to open the door to her hotel room.

"Are you okay?" Henrik asked, gently.

"I'm fine," Jo said, flicking on the light and hoping her voice didn't shake.

"Look, I don't mind sitting and talking," Henrik said, following her into the room. "I'm not expecting anything, and truth be told, I was enjoying our conversation. I'm definitely not looking for anything ongoing."

Jo smiled and shut the door. "I appreciate you telling me that. I'm not interested in that either."

"I won't lie. I did enjoy the kiss as well as the conversation."

Warmth spread across her cheeks. "I did as well."

Henrik moved closer to her, and her breath caught in her throat, her pulse racing.

"Did you, now?" he asked, softly.

"I-it's been some time…" she stammered nervously.

Henrik reached out and brushed his knuckles gently on her cheek again. Heat flooded her body. All that fear she had been feeling melted away.

She needed this. She wanted to feel something, to live again so that, maybe one day, she wouldn't be so scared if Mr. Right came along again, though she seriously doubted that would happen.

She wasn't that lucky.

Henrik was here, right now, and it had been a long time since she had been so attracted to someone.

She wanted this. She wanted him.

For just one night.

The first step in finding herself again.

"How about that drink?" he asked, his voice deep, husky and full of promise.

"I don't actually have anything," she whispered. Now she was trembling for a whole other reason, and she strengthened her resolve to be with him tonight.

He grinned, his eyes twinkling in the dim light of the room.

"Your lips are good enough for me."

It was a corny line, but she fell for it. The first time she had kissed him she'd felt a jolt of electricity. Now, with him kissing her, her body turned into a live wire. Like she was being woken up after a long sleep.

This is what she needed.

One night of passion.

She didn't need forever. She'd thought she'd had that once, and she was never going to risk her heart for a forever again.

CHAPTER TWO

One month later

JO WAS TRYING to ignore the little stick on the edge of the bathroom sink. It just confirmed her thoughts that doctors do indeed sometimes make the worst patients. All she wanted to do was hurry the test up. She needed the answer right now.

And she was feeling very antsy waiting for that timer to go off.

It couldn't be positive. It just couldn't be.

Jo worried her bottom lip and stared at her watch. Only a minute left.

It had to be a stomach bug. There was a stomach bug that had been going through Nubbin's Harbor, thanks to a tourist who had spread it to the unwitting residents en route to Tilting. For the last couple of weeks Jo had been dealing with a stomach virus that had run rampant through all her patients.

Not much to be done except prescribe fluids and rest.

Everyone seemed to be sick, but Jo thought it had been tapering off; then she'd started to feel nauseated and dizzy at times. Some niggling thought told her it wasn't the virus, and yet she had never been so busy: she was even getting patients in from farther afield because the hospital emergency room was full. It couldn't be pregnancy. It just couldn't be. The only time she'd had sex since David died was a month ago with Henrik.

A warm flush spread though her body at just the thought of Henrik. Her mysterious stranger with the blue, blue eyes and kisses that made her melt.

Even though it had been a one-time only thing, she couldn't stop thinking about him. The way his lips felt on hers, the touch of those skilled hands on her skin.

She tried not to think about him, but every time she walked through Nubbin's Harbor she'd look for him, hoping to see him again, which frustrated her. He'd told her he was leaving. Had she expected him to come back for her?

She wasn't here for romance. She was here to work.

Still, their one night together had been electric, but that didn't mean she was pregnant. They had used protection.

Protection isn't one hundred percent reliable.

Jo cursed under her breath. She had told that to so many others before.

She knew one thing: if she was pregnant, then she was pregnant. It was as simple as that. She'd always wanted children. It was something she and David had always planned for. It was something they had tried for, for over a year, but it turned out that they had unexplained infertility. Every month her heart was broken, and David would remind her that everything was okay. All through the pain from IVF that she'd endured, he had held her hand.

She'd known it would happen for them one day. It was what she'd held on to.

And David had always convinced her of that. When he died, Jo really thought that was it. She would never be a mother now, because she couldn't see herself being with anyone again.

Until that night with Henrik.

Who'd left the next morning.

Jo hadn't regretted that act of impulsivity. It was one more step toward getting her life back, and that night had been wonderful.

It just tore at her heart that the baby wasn't and couldn't be David's the way she'd hoped for from the moment she'd married him.

The baby she'd mourned when she'd buried her husband.

You're getting ahead of yourself. It's probably just a stomach bug.

The thought of a baby made her stomach flutter with hope and excitement. No, a baby with a stranger wasn't ideal or anything close to what she'd imagined for herself, but she would still be ecstatic if she was pregnant.

A child. Her son or daughter.

Something she'd always wanted yet tried not to wish for too often.

The timer went off, and she picked up the pregnancy test. Her hand was shaking, and it took her a moment to register the fact that there were two pink lines staring up at her, rather than one.

It was definitely not a stomach bug. Although right at this moment a part of her wanted to throw up, there was another, much larger part that was absolutely thrilled that she was going to have a baby.

Before David died, they had used their last embryo, and it hadn't been viable.

They were going to try again, but he'd died before they could, and with his death her dream had sputtered away.

This pregnancy felt like a miracle.

Tears stung her eyes, and she smiled as she stared down at the stick.

She knew when she came to work in Newfoundland for the year that she was looking for a change, she just never expected that it would be this big. Her mind started to whirl about what she was going to do, but she was sure that her mother would come up from Arizona and help her for a bit.

She chuckled softly to herself that her father's dreams about retirement in Arizona might come to a screeching halt with the impending birth of a grandchild.

You're getting ahead of yourself.

Jo took another calming breath and lay the stick down, washing her hands and then splashing some cold water on her face. She was only a month in; something awful could happen. It had happened to her before, when she and David had first started trying…

"Jo?" David had opened the door to the bathroom, and his face had fallen when he'd seen her on the floor.

"I'm sorry," she'd cried.

David had knelt down. "It's okay. I told you, when it happens, you're going to be an excellent mother. I know it."

"I'm not sure about that," she'd sniffed.

David had touched her face, wiping away her tears. "I am."

Jo swallowed the lump in her throat. It was too soon to get her hopes up.

She reached down and gingerly cupped her abdomen.

Stay with me, little one, she begged. Just wanting to hold on to something which still seemed so intangible.

The door chimed as someone walked into the clinic.

"Doc?" they called.

She recognized Lloyd's voice.

She brushed away the tears and straightened her hair. "Coming!"

Jo left the bathroom and smiled at him.

"Lloyd, how can I help you?" she asked.

"It's not me, but there's been an accident in Tilting. A bad one, out at sea, and they're requesting all medical personnel to come as quick as they can.

I'm with the volunteer firefighters here, so I can take you."

Jo nodded. "Of course. Just give me five minutes to grab what I need, and I'll meet you outside."

Lloyd nodded grimly and left the clinic.

Jo grabbed all the emergency gear that she had prepared for when the village would be inundated with tourists for iceberg season.

When Gary had talked to her about his practice, he'd mentioned that there were often tourists that would get too close to these massive behemoths of ice and slip. Just trying to get that perfect picture.

And then there were the fishers who were out shrimping and crabbing. Some of the locals even harvested sea cucumbers, and the sea was not always a kind mistress. The sea didn't care what you fished, legally or illegally when it claimed lives.

Gary had told her it was wise to have emergency kits prepared.

So that's exactly what she did.

Fogo had a hospital, but it was always best to be prepared. She'd learned that during her years as a trauma surgeon. She had first learned family medicine, but liked the fast pace of the hospital emergency room more.

Both her experiences would come in handy today.

Jennifer, her receptionist, came into the supply room to help her with the bags.

"I'll cancel the rest of the patients for the day," she said.

"Thanks, Jenn. I appreciate that."

"There weren't that many, really. Most are still out sick with that stomach bug and called in to reschedule."

"I would be lost without you." Which was true. Jennifer was a native to Fogo and had been a huge help in welcoming Jo here.

Jo was thankful for the friend.

Jennifer helped her carry the bags outside.

She shut the door to her clinic as Lloyd took the trauma bags and hefted them into the back of his small truck.

"Will there be paramedics there?" she asked, climbing into the front seat.

"Aye, and the coast guard. When I got the call, I told them that I would be bringing you."

"Do you know what happened?" she asked, as Lloyd drove the short distance to Tilting.

"Aye, pirates."

Normally, if anyone else would've said that to her, she would've given them a look of derision, but Lloyd was stone-cold serious.

And after kissing a cod a month ago, it didn't seem too far-fetched.

"Pirates?" she echoed.

"Well, not real pirates, but boys that were out fishing illegally. *Jigging* we call it. There's a moratorium on who can fish cod here. They're not from

Fogo but were going to sell it on the black market. They got into a chase with the coast guard, and their ship exploded."

"Exploded?" she asked, trying to process in her brain how a ship could explode at sea.

"Aye." Lloyd nodded. "The paramedics and the coast guard are a wee bit overwhelmed, pulling the bodies from the water and dealing with the wreckage."

Jo pursed her lips.

A sea faring vessel exploding was not a trauma that she was familiar with, though she had seen her share of combustion injuries. They were probably dealing with drownings, burns and most likely internal or shrapnel injuries.

Going over what she could possibly have to deal with helped her focus on what she had to do. Trying to always think three steps ahead was why she was one of the best trauma surgeons in Toronto, but it was the fast pace that had also threatened to burn her out.

When they rounded the corner, she could see the smoke rising over the rocky outcrops. She actually gasped out loud the closer they got to the shoreline. The coast guard was out there dealing with the fire, but there was also a stream of smaller boats and divers dealing with the injured and the bodies.

There were several ambulances and makeshift

trauma and morgue areas set up. She could see bodies covered in blankets on the beach.

"How big was the boat that exploded?" she asked.

"Large. Such a waste of life. And a waste of cod too," Lloyd grumbled.

Lloyd might lack tact, but since cod fishing had been their way of life for so long and it had been taken away, she could understand his bitterness at the loss of the fish. "Who should I report to?"

"I'll find ma b'y, Rik, who is in charge of this. He'll get you sorted."

Lloyd parked, and they got out of the truck and grabbed the gear. Lloyd started gesticulating and shouted, "Whaddaya at, Rik! I've brought the doc!"

There was a group of coast-guard paramedics on shore. Rik turned to wave back to Lloyd, and that's when her world stopped turning as she stared at the paramedic who was in charge. A lump formed in her throat, and she felt again like she was going to be sick.

At least he looked as shocked as her, as he came closer.

Her one-night stand.

The father of her baby.

Henrik.

The man who'd told her he was leaving the island for work, and she'd assumed he'd meant he was gone for good.

"Rik, this is Doc Jo, as we all call her now, but

then you should know her. You were there the night she came to Nubbin's Harbor."

Henrik's blue eyes settled on hers, and her heart skipped a beat. Her body reacted viscerally to the sight of him, warmth spreading through her as flashes of sensual memories of that night raced through her mind.

It was hard to find any words.

She'd only wanted one night with him, yet standing here now all she wanted to do was leap into his arms and melt.

You can't. That's not why you're here.

"You're Doc Jo?" he asked, interrupting her thoughts with the intense shock in his tone.

"The one and the same," she said, finding her voice.

It looked like he wanted to say more. A lot more. "Good, we need all the help we can get. I'll show you where to start."

"Lead the way... Rik."

There was no time to talk about what had happened a month ago, or how she'd thought he wasn't coming back, or why she hadn't seen him since that night, or how she couldn't stop thinking about him.

None of that mattered now.

She had a job to do.

Henrik was completely floored to discover the doctor he'd heard so much about was not called Joseph, as he'd assumed, but rather Josephine, the woman that he had been thinking about for the entire month he'd been away.

It had bothered him that he couldn't get her out of his head. Usually one-night stands were just that—done and dusted.

It had been some time since he'd been this pre-occupied thinking about a woman he had been intimate with. Dreaming about her kisses, the way she'd sighed in his arms, her velvety-soft skin and the scent of her hair.

Even just recalling it again now made his pulse quicken.

He'd planned to throw himself into his work when he arrived back home and forget all about her. He'd thought she was a tourist and would be long gone, and usually work helped to get his mind off his paramours. It always had with the others, even Melissa.

Seeing Josephine, he knew his plan was obviously not going to work. The siren that had been haunting him for weeks while he was at sea was here.

In the flesh.

The new doctor of the community. Someone that he would have to deal with on a regular basis, given that he was a first responder here. Was karma finally getting back at him? His gran always used to say that his recklessness and his hardened heart would bite him in the backside one day. Not that he'd ever been mean or cruel to anyone. His gran had just never approved of his *philandering ways*, as she'd called it.

He'd thought it was just her usual ramblings, but then, his grandmother had never really been wrong.

"The arse is gone out of 'er, my boy, if you keep at this with the come from aways!"

Basically, she was warning him that all was going to go to hell in a handbag if he kept playing around with tourists. He knew that Gran had wanted him to settle down, but after Melissa it was far too hard to even contemplate opening his heart to a woman again. And he certainly was never going to settle down with someone east of the Rock.

His home was here.

This was where he'd been born and raised. Everyone else had left to find work on the mainland, and he wouldn't risk his heart on another person who would leave.

Fogo owned his heart.

Still, Josephine had been in his thoughts, and for one brief moment he'd even wished that she hadn't been a come from away. He'd wished she was staying.

Now, here she was, staying. She was the new doctor, and part of him was incredibly happy about that, but the loudest part of his soul was telling him to run. To keep away. Josephine was a serious threat to his damaged heart, and he wasn't sure that he could deal with such heartache again.

There was some shouting, and he shook his head,

snapping himself out of his thoughts. Josephine was standing in front of him, her finely arched brow cocked, waiting.

Right.

Accident.

"Follow me," he said, gruffly, annoyed at himself for zoning out. That was not something he did in situations like this. He had to get control of himself and his emotions. There was a job to do here, lives on the line.

He made his way down to where they had set up a triage area for those who'd survived the explosion. There had apparently been a crew of twenty onboard, and only ten had been recovered so far, with five of them having perished.

"We're tagging those that need to be taken by ambulance right away." He handed her some tags. "Do what you can, as we only have so many ambulances on the island to take them to hospital. The diving teams are still working on retrieving those in the water."

Josephine paled. "Right."

"You okay? Have you worked trauma before?" he asked.

"I was a trauma surgeon in Toronto," she said stiffly, pulling on her rubber gloves. "I can handle this."

"Are you sure? You looked like you were going to be sick."

Her spine stiffened. "Oh? And you can diagnose that from a glance?"

"Some people can't stand the sight of trauma."

"I'm a physician and a surgeon, and I've seen explosions before in the city. I can deal." Josephine made her way to one of the injured on the ground and started her checks on the survivors. Henrik headed back to the shore as another dinghy came in.

He helped another paramedic as they took a backboard down to the dinghy. The moment he got close he could see the survivor was bleeding out, his femoral artery cut, and the diver was applying pressure to the wound with a towel.

"We have a trauma surgeon triaging," Henrik said, quickly directing the other paramedic to take the man to where Josephine was working. She looked up as they got closer, and he didn't even have to call her over. She could see exactly what the issue was.

"Femoral artery?" she asked, leaning over to check the patient's vitals.

"Yes. If he doesn't stabilize, he won't make it to the hospital," Henrik answered grimly.

"Okay." Josephine pursed her lips. "We're going to do this in the back of an ambulance. I need lots of light, and it'll be more sanitary in there than out here."

Henrik nodded and helped guide the unconscious patient into the back of the ambulance on a stretcher. As the man was secured, Henrik set up a large-bore IV to get fluids into him, while Josephine readied what she needed.

The diver was still applying pressure to the wound, but the towel was soaking through with blood.

Josephine had a clamp ready as they removed the towel.

Henrik leaned over. "Tell me what you need."

"Hold the light still," she directed.

She just nodded in acknowledgment as he did and she clamped the vein to stop the bleeding. "I think that I can suture the artery so that it will hold until he gets to the hospital. Can the Fogo Island Hospital handle a vascular surgery?" she asked.

"He'll be flown to St. John's from there," Henrik stated. "He just needs to make it to the hospital."

"We'll get him there. You have a suture kit?"

Henrik pulled out a kit, and Josephine went to work, getting her tools ready to sew up the artery so that the patient could be transported.

"Start some antibiotics," Josephine said as she cleaned the wound. "If he was in the water, he'll need it, but I'm also concerned about what cut his leg. I don't know what shrapnel from the explosion did this."

"I have cefazolin," Henrik said, going through the medicine that was on hand.

"That'll be fine." Josephine continued her careful work. Cleaning and repairing what she could so the patient had his best shot at survival. Henrik watched in amazement. He had seen trauma surgeons before, but not in the field like this.

Not when there was chaos around them, and doing such a delicate repair in the back of an ambulance. It was like they were in this small bubble of their own in the back of the vehicle, just them working together over the patient.

It took him straight back to the first night they met. When their eyes had locked, he'd almost felt he'd been looking back at the other half of his soul.

And now, here, watching her work, it was calm.

A life was being saved right in front of him.

They shared the same passion. He'd never met anyone quite like her before, which was probably the reason he'd had such a hard time forgetting her. She was a danger to his carefully guarded heart.

"There," Josephine said. "Let's pack this wound and get him off to the hospital."

Henrik handed her what she needed to pack and then cover it. He readied the patient for transport as Josephine disposed of the suture kit and her rubber gloves. She climbed out of the back of the ambulance and called the Fogo Island Hospital.

Telling them exactly what to expect so they could call in the correct surgeon or have the air ambulance ready to whisk him to St. John's.

Henrik helped close the back doors of the ambulance and banged on the back, signaling to the driver that they could leave.

Josephine stepped back as the lights flipped on and the sirens blared.

"That was impressive work," Henrik stated. "I haven't seen a femoral repair in the field."

"It wasn't really a repair. He'll need much more work, and he isn't out of the woods yet. I'm sure the vascular surgeon in charge will cringe at my handiwork. There's a reason we're referred to as the *meatballers* of the surgical world."

"I've always found that distinction quite unjust."

She smiled at him. "Well, let's go check on the others. The divers are still bringing victims in."

Henrik nodded.

He stood there and watched her head back to the triage area, where there were more survivors being loaded into ambulances.

On the other side of the beach, there were far too many bodies, and he was mad that it had come down to this. To this desperation to make money. It cost lives, and he hated it, but the one thing he didn't detest was Josephine being here.

At first, seeing her there, he'd experienced a fleeting moment of panic.

When he'd first met her a month ago, the come-from-away woman he'd spent the night with, he'd thought she was a delicate flower. How wrong he had been. Just watching her throw herself into the fray of this emergency situation had seriously impressed him.

Don't think like that. Don't let her impress you.

He had to be careful.

He had to keep her at a distance.

It was bad enough that he couldn't stop thinking about her for the month he'd been on his training mission.

Now she was close enough to put his heart on the line again, and that was something he wasn't willing to do because she wasn't from here. She'd leave eventually.

Just like Melissa.

Like so many others.

There were no ties for Josephine here, and to protect himself from pain he couldn't offer her any reason to stay.

Even though part of him secretly wanted to.

CHAPTER THREE

HENRIK HAD MANAGED to skirt her for the rest of the time they were at the beach. He'd had to trade off and head out into the water to do retrieval of the victims. It was always the hardest part of the job for him, being in the water.

His parents had been lost at sea.

Their bodies were never recovered. It was difficult not to think about how the water was so dangerous. How fast it could turn and steal a life. There was always a moment of sheer terror when he headed out into the water, but also clarity. Henrik always went into the water thinking he'd do the best job he could. He was beating the sea by working hard to save lives. His own form of revenge. His own way of honoring the memory of his parents.

So that's what he did.

Focusing on that helped him briefly forget about Josephine's presence on shore.

At the end of the day, from a crew of twenty men, there were only twelve survivors and by some kind of miracle they had managed to retrieve all the bodies.

Now the coast guard had to deal with the ramifications of the accident and lay criminal charges on those involved, but that was not part of his job. He was off duty, and all he had to do was head back to his place and put this whole thing out of his mind.

Yeah. Good luck with that.

Henrik threw his gear in the back of his truck, but as he surveyed the area one last time before he left, he saw Josephine standing there, searching for someone. He should just let her be, only he couldn't. She looked a little lost, like that first day he'd met her, just a bit more tired and wrung-out.

"Looking for someone?" he asked. One part of him hoping that it was him and the other, louder part hoping it wasn't.

They'd had a one-night stand. He couldn't give her more.

He wouldn't.

"Lloyd brought me here, but he's disappeared."

"Ah, yes… Lloyd is a great volunteer, but sometimes he's the first out of a situation. That and the pub is about to open for the night. I'm sorry he forgot about you."

"He was my ride back to Nubbin's Harbor." She frowned.

"Well, I'm heading back there. I can take you home. Though, I don't know where you're living now."

"I need to go to the clinic. I have some stuff to clean up. And I live above it."

"In Gary's… I mean, Dr. Linwood's place?" Henrik asked.

"Yes. I'm here for the next year, covering for him while he teaches in Munich."

So she wasn't a tourist passing through. That much he had gathered, but there was still an expiry date to her time on Fogo.

Just as he'd thought.

"I had no idea Dr. Linwood had even left."

"Did you know Gary well?"

Henrik frowned and rubbed the back of his neck. "Can't say that I did, to be honest. I mean, we worked together on occasion, but he wasn't one for socializing much with the bayfolk or townies."

"You mean the *locals*?" she asked.

"You're starting to pick up the slang?" he asked, secretly pleased.

Josephine hefted her gear. "How could I not, living here for a month and being the talk of the harbor by kissing a cod on my very first night? That and Jennifer Wells, my receptionist, has been helpful."

Henrik took her bags from her. "Aye, well that would make an impression. I'll try to slow down some for you."

"I would appreciate that, and thanks for offering me the ride. I probably could've walked. It's not that far. Or I could've called Jenn. Just thought of that."

"It's twenty kilometers, and it's getting dark," he said. The thought of being alone with her again was tantalizing, but it was not the smartest thing.

How could he get Josephine out of his mind so

they could have a professional relationship if he spent too much time alone with her?

Still, he couldn't abandon her without a ride. He wouldn't.

"It can't be that dangerous. Or not as dangerous as walking up Yonge Street at night." There was a nervous edge to her voice.

"Well, maybe not, but you've only been here a month, and you're still a come from away. You're not local. There's also moose. You don't want to deal with them." He opened the door of the truck for her, and she climbed in.

He closed the door and then climbed into the driver's side. His pulse was thundering between his ears. He just had to focus on the road and make idle chatter.

Just because they'd shared one mind-blowing night of ecstasy didn't mean they couldn't be professional acquaintances.

And back his mind wandered to that night and the taste of her on his tongue...

He needed to get ahold of himself.

"Moose aren't predators," she said, dryly as he started the engine.

"No, but they're seriously big, and they know it. Have you ever seen a car accident involving a moose?"

"No, but I did hear of them. You don't get many moose accidents in Toronto's emergency departments."

He chuckled. "No, I suppose not."

She looked away, and silence fell.

He drove away from the scene of the accident and headed back on the highway. Back through Joe Batt's Arm and toward Nubbin's Harbor. Even though he had to go away from time to time for work, it was always good to be home.

Especially with summer on the horizon.

He liked the late sunsets. The vibrant colors of the houses poised on the rocks.

The blue of the sea.

Nubbin's Harbor was a small community of houses, the pub, the hotel, the diner, the clinic and a handful of shops. The colors alternated between red and white. They were clustered together around a tiny natural harbor that used to have a fishing industry but now was empty.

The old lighthouse was out on the farthest spit of land, and attached to it was a faded yellow house.

His late gran's. Now his.

It was home.

And he'd missed it. He was glad to be back at work. It kept the loneliness away.

He couldn't help but wonder what Josephine thought of Fogo. Most visitors loved the charm, for a short time. Fogo was still fairly isolated. They hadn't even gotten electricity until the midsixties. If they weren't born there, they rarely stayed.

That was his belief.

Even Dr. Linwood left.

He glanced over at her and saw she was wringing her hands nervously. A flush on her face.

He loved the pink on her round cheeks.

"I have to say, I was surprised to see you," he said, breaking the tense silence that had fallen between them. "I thought you were just passing through, as most do."

"I never said that I was, but we didn't talk much about that. Besides, I thought you were leaving the island for work reasons and not coming back."

Another blush tinged her cheeks afresh, and his pulse quickened again. She was so gorgeous, just as beautiful as he remembered. He thought he had built it up in his mind how stunning she was.

He hadn't.

There was something about her that he couldn't quite put his finger on. Something that drew him in, and he didn't like it.

"This is my home. I'm about as local as you can get to Fogo. Generations of my family have lived and worked here."

And he was all that was left here, only he didn't tell her that. There was no need to.

He had to stay.

He couldn't abandon his home. This is where he belonged. Even if it meant being alone for the rest of his life.

"You're a paramedic, so you had a sabbatical? Is that why you were away for a month?" she asked curiously.

"I'm a first responder as well, and I volunteer with sea search and rescue, so I go on training missions with the coast guard. They bring in cadets from all over Canada, maybe even some who didn't grow up by the sea, and put them through training. I assist with that from time to time. I have a lot of experience in dealing with sea ice and rescues in northern waters."

Josephine's eyes widened. "Wow. That's impressive."

Henrik shrugged. "It's my passion. Saving those who are lost at sea."

"They can't be gone, Gran," he'd whispered. "Da knew the sea."

"I know, my b'y. I know." Her hand had been on his shoulder, giving it a squeeze. "Come on, let's go home."

"No. I want to stay here. I promised to wait for them."

"Then, I'll stay with you. Right here."

He knew firsthand the pain of losing family to the sea. The gut-wrenching pain, which felt like your heart was being ripped out of your chest still beating, some days felt raw. Never knowing what had happened, never recovering their bodies.

They were just lost.

He'd been twelve and gone to live with his gran and grandad at the lighthouse, but he still hated the sea sometimes for swallowing up his whole world and shaping his life in such a painful way. It's why he did what he did.

His own form of revenge against the sea, saving as many of those as he could, who might otherwise be lost.

"Well, that explains why you've been away, then," she said softly, and when he glanced over at her, she was wringing her hands and worrying her bottom lip.

"Look, I'm not looking for a relationship... especially with someone I'm working with," he said abruptly. "So if that's what you're worrying about..."

She looked confused. "That's not even close to what I was thinking when I asked where you've been or why you've been away."

"Usually, that's why women ask. I'm not looking for anything long-term. Which I mentioned the night we met."

Her eyes narrowed. "And I believe I said the same thing to you. I'm only here for a year, Henrik. And I've already had my great love. I'm not interested in anything else."

The reference to her loss piqued his interest.

He'd had that great love too. Or so he'd thought. He'd certainly had enough heartache. He knew he had seen something in her eyes the night they'd met.

She'd experienced pain and loss like him.

"Yes. I feel the same," he said, softly.

"Right." There was sympathy in her gaze.

He wondered what had really brought her here and why she'd left Toronto to help out a friend.

"Then…"

"I was getting to know you and…" She trailed off nervously. "There's no easy way to tell you this, Henrik, and honestly if you were a stranger passing through, it would be a moot point anyway. But since you're from here and we'll be seeing each other around… I mean Nubbin's Harbor isn't exactly a metropolis, is it?"

"You're rambling."

"I know." Josephine folded her hands in her lap. It reminded him of every doctor that was about to deliver bad news to a patient. "I'm pregnant, Henrik. And the baby is yours."

His heart stopped beating, and he had to pull over to the side of the road, because if he didn't he was going to crash the truck. His hands gripped the wheel, his knuckles locking as he tried to process exactly what she was saying to him.

Pregnant?

He'd dreamed of having a family once. When he'd thought he and Melissa were going to get married. For that brief moment, he thought he'd get back that happy family he'd lost.

Then Melissa had left.

It reminded him that loving only brought pain. So he'd given up on the dream of ever becoming a father.

He still couldn't believe what Josephine was telling him.

"We used protection," he mumbled. He had one-night stands, but he wasn't a fool.

"And that's not always reliable. You know that."

His tongue felt thick against the roof of his mouth, and it was hard to swallow. It was almost impossible to hear what she was actually saying.

Josephine was pregnant? With his child?

He didn't know what he was going to do.

He didn't know how to react. All he could do was stare out, utterly shocked, through the windshield over Nubbin's Harbor as his gran's words about his sleeping around replayed in his mind.

Yeah, he'd made a right arse of this whole situation.

When she was nervous she rambled. It was a quirk she hated about herself. The last person she had expected to see today was Henrik, but here he was.

And the whole time she'd worked triage on the beach, she was thinking about how she was going to tell him she was pregnant.

So when he'd offered her a ride home, it just came out. Jo was regretting telling him while they were driving, but he was insinuating that she was looking for a relationship with him, and that was the last thing she wanted. When she'd got together with him a month ago, she was just taking a leap into getting her life back.

The last thing she wanted was a relationship with anyone.

Honestly, she hadn't really come to terms with it completely herself since the stick turned positive, right before the boat accident. And the last thing she'd ever have expected was to run into the one man she had had a fling with.

The father of her surprise.

She'd really thought she'd never see Henrik again. Even though she was terrified at the prospect of being a single mother, she wanted this baby more than anything. It was a dream come true. It was her body and her choice, but she wasn't going to deny Henrik his child. Like it or not, if he chose to be involved with the baby, he was in her life for good.

"Look, trust me, I'm just as taken aback as you, and I really don't expect anything from you. I can take care of this child by myself. A baby was not in my plans for my year here, but I can manage."

Henrik didn't say anything but nodded a couple of times, before he straightened in his seat. "I want to be a part of my child's life."

"Good!"

Henrik nodded again but still seemed to be in some sort of daze.

"Do you need me to drive?" Jo asked.

Henrik chuckled hoarsely. "Nah, I'm fine."

"You're sure?"

"Aye. As fine as I'll ever be." He turned the ignition, and they got back on the road, back down to Nubbin's Harbor. "We need to talk more about this and not on the side of the road."

"Agreed."

It wasn't an ideal location, telling him in his truck, but she really had just wanted to get it out there and let him know what had happened. He had the right to know, and she really couldn't hold it back for long.

"Would you like to have dinner at my place?" he asked. "I have a nice roast in my slow cooker. I usually eat alone, but I think we have a lot to discuss."

"That sounds good."

And she was quite hungry.

Henrik nodded and didn't say much more as they drove through town and down a winding gravel road that made its way out onto a thin spit of rock and land at the edge of the ocean. There was a small, run-down lighthouse that was no longer in operation.

The little cottage attached to it was yellow. It reminded her of a bright sunny day. She'd often wondered who lived in this place.

"You live in the lighthouse?"

"I do. My great-grandad was a lighthouse keeper. When it was decommissioned, my gran bought it. It was her father's place, where she grew up. When Gran died two years ago, it became mine."

"I thought the town would want it as a historical site," Jo said. "The lighthouses in Ontario are like that."

Henrik chuckled. "Not here."

Henrik parked his truck. He got out and opened the passenger-side door for her, taking her hand in his strong one to help her down, treating her like she was some fragile vessel that was about to break.

Although, she really wasn't going to complain. David had treated her a bit like that, in their tender moments together. It was nice that it gave her that memory, but it also reminded her that she was finally getting her family despite it not being David. She had a fleeting thought that maybe she and Henrik could eventually have something more.

You don't know him. He's a stranger.

And that thought sobered her. Henrik wasn't David.

Her husband had been someone incredibly special.

Henrik was just a polite, kind man she'd slept with once. She barely knew him. Just because he had certain similarities to David didn't mean anything in the long run.

Henrik's family home was like all the other clapboard houses that dotted Fogo Island. Its bright yellow paint was different from the reds and blues that she had seen since she'd arrived in Newfoundland, but it was bright and cheerful in the setting late-spring sun.

"Gran liked yellow," Henrik offered. "Everyone always comments on it. It's like a large lemon."

"I wasn't going to say anything," Jo said. "It seems to suit it."

He smiled, those blue eyes twinkling at her just like they had a month ago. "Well, I often get asked why I live in a yellow house. Why I live in a cottage that should be for a little old lady."

"Who says that?" she asked.

"Some of the well-meaning saucy women in town. 'Oh, lover, you should really think about sprucing up your home. 'tis not fit for a man like you.'"

Jo's eyes widened. "The ladies in town call you *lover*?"

Henrik laughed. "No, it doesn't mean the same thing when it's said in a syrupy, condescending tone. It's meant as a form of endearment. Like *dearie*. Not everyone says it, but a few women around Nubbin's Harbor do. Most people refer to others as *ducky*."

"Oh, I was going to ask if you were some kind of Fogo Island playboy," she teased.

"Only with the come from aways. Never the bayfolk." He smiled, that same devious smile that had won her over a month ago. Although, Jo was still adamant that it wasn't his charm but rather the screech that had done it. She chuckled to herself at that thought.

No, she couldn't blame the drink. She had definitely been drawn to him before her screech-in.

He opened the door to his house.

The scent of the roast beef that he had in his slow cooker made her stomach growl the moment she stepped into the mudroom. She was nervous stepping into Henrik's world. It was incredibly intimate.

Even more so than a hotel room.

Henrik took her coat, his fingers brushing her shoulders which sent a thrill down her spine.

"Smells wonderful in here," she said, hoping her voice didn't shake.

"Ta," he said. "I do enjoy cooking."

She was impressed that he could cook. David hadn't been much for cooking, and she was a bit of a disaster in the kitchen herself.

"How is it?" she had asked.

David had smiled, but she'd been able to tell he was overchewing, and the smile hadn't reached his eyes.

"It's good."

"You're lying. It's spaghetti. It's not hard."

"Oh…you're wrong. It's definitely hard."

"What?" she'd asked, horrified.

"*Crunchy* is more like it."

Josephine smiled as the memory faded away.

Henrik slipped off his coat and hung it up with hers, as she kicked off her shoes.

"Make yourself at home. I'm going to start a fire to get some heat going, and dinner should be ready soon." Henrik disappeared around the corner, and she heard the back door shut.

Jo made her way into the tiny parlor that had vintage furniture and crocheted afghans. She could see why the women of Nubbin's Harbor were concerned about him living in his grandparents' home. It certainly didn't scream *bachelor* or *young man*.

Still, it was homey.

And she felt comfortable here. It put her at ease when, inside, she was just a jangle of nerves.

She looked at various family pictures. Black-and-white grainy photographs of the lighthouse when it was functional, and men with catches of fish. It was like a family history, a tapestry, on the faded floral wallpaper that lined the home.

She had family pictures somewhere. In a box, in her storage unit.

Her place in Toronto had been functional and minimalistic.

There was something cozy and eclectic about Henrik's place.

The door in the back opened, and he peered around the corner. "The fire is lit. Are you hungry?"

"Yes."

Jo made her way to the kitchen, which surprised her: it was so modern and updated compared to the rest of the house. This felt more like a successful bachelor's place. All modern and clean.

"I'm renovating," Henrik said, pulling out two

plates from the cupboard. "The house is a work in progress, and Gran's kitchen still had a coal stove, so it had to be done first. Just in case you're wondering about the decor elsewhere."

Jo laughed. "I'm sure your work keeps you busy."

"It does." He set down the plates at the table. "Have a seat. Everything is in one pot, as it were. The beef, the potatoes and carrots."

"It smells wonderful. Thank you for inviting me over and sharing your dinner with me."

"It's no problem." Henrik served up the meal. The roast was so tender he didn't even have to cut it. It seemed to fall apart on the serving platter. Once he had everything out of his slow cooker, he set the platter on the table. "I would offer you wine, but I don't think that's wise. I have bottled water."

She nodded. "Water is great."

Henrik got her a bottle from the fridge and one for himself. He served her food first and then took some for himself. Jo couldn't remember the last time she'd sat down at a meal like this. Probably when her own grandparents had been alive.

"You're smiling so dreamily," Henrik said. "Am I that good of a cook?"

"Sorry! Yes, it's delicious, but I was just thinking of my own grandmother and her house. Your living room reminded me a bit of a time capsule."

Henrik smiled. "It is, but I'm having a hard time parting with it. It reminds me so much of my gran. Still, it'll eventually be renovated."

"I can understand that. You had her in your life for a long time."

"When did your grandmother die?" he asked.

"When I was fourteen, and then the year after, we buried my grandfather. I swear he died of a broken heart. I know that's a silly thing to say, but he just gave up."

And then the memory hit her from nowhere.

"Jo, you can't lie here all day. You have work to get back to," her mother had said softly. "David would want you to continue on."

"It's easy enough to say but not to do," she'd murmured.

After his death, she hadn't been able to bring herself to get up out of bed. It had felt like she had a gaping wound in her chest and her life was over. What was there to live for?

"Don't be like my father. Please," her mother had said, her voice catching. "Live. David would want you to live."

Only, she hadn't felt like living at that moment.

She'd wanted to be with David and not live alone with their shattered dreams.

"I could believe dying of a broken heart," Henrik said thoughtfully, continuing on with the conversation and jarring her from her thoughts.

There was that connection between them again. The shared pain as if he knew grief in the same way she did.

"Could you?" she asked, as she swallowed the tears that were threatening to spill.

"Yes. Almost thought my gran would die when my grandad did. She held on, but she was never the same."

She understood that all too well.

It made her uncomfortable to think about the struggle it had been to hold on after David died.

"Well, we're not here to talk about that," she said, trying to steer the conversation away from broken hearts and shattered dreams.

There was a life growing inside her that they had to discuss.

"Right. The baby," Henrik said stiffly.

"Yes. As I said, I can take full responsibility. I kind of sprung this on you, and we didn't make any promises to each other that night. So you can be as involved as you want. It's up to you. I'm not expecting anything."

Henrik frowned. "Aye, but I do take full responsibility. It is my child too."

"Yes." She was glad that he wanted to be in their child's life. She wasn't sure how it was all going to work out when she left Newfoundland and returned to Ontario, but they'd be able to organize some kind of custody arrangement. "Thank you for being so understanding."

Henrik nodded. "So do you think we ought to get married?"

CHAPTER FOUR

Jo ALMOST CHOKED on the mouthful of water she'd just taken. Now it was her turn to be stunned. She coughed and then swallowed the hard lump of panic that was suddenly lodged in her throat.

"You think we should get married?"

Henrik winced. "Isn't that what's expected?"

"Maybe if this was like…fifty years ago. Henrik, I don't want to get married. Do you want to get married?"

He frowned. "No. I don't. It's why I only usually get involved with tourists. I don't want or have time for a relationship."

It sounded a little callous, but she understood: she didn't want a relationship either. Even though her one night with Henrik had been amazing, it wasn't enough to build a permanent future on.

There had to be more than just amazing sex.

"Right." She rolled her eyes. "So you've told me. Look, we can work out raising this child together and not have to marry each other. You should love your partner when you choose to enter into that kind of commitment."

She knew that firsthand.

She had loved David. So much.

Marriage was something she had never really wanted until she'd met David. She'd been so happy with him. Until it all came crashing down. There was a part of her that was nervous about raising this baby on her own and trying to balance a very full career as a trauma surgeon in a Toronto hospital with parenting a child, but she was up to the task. Although she'd always pictured having a traditional family, life clearly had other plans for her.

Her baby would still have two parents.

Henrik was on board with being a part of their baby's life. It was just going to look a little different and span two provinces when her friend came back from Germany and she would have to leave Nubbin's Harbor.

Then a terrible thought crept into her mind. What if Henrik didn't allow her to leave with their child? What if he sued for custody? She hated to think this way about him, but she didn't know him well enough yet.

He was the father of her baby and still really a stranger to her.

You can make it work.

She wanted to be friends with Henrik, and she also had to work with him. She was letting her anxiety get the better of her. They had to make this work.

Of course, the one man she had been attracted to since David died, the one person she decided to have an uncharacteristic one-night stand with was a colleague. Fate was cruel.

"You're right. I wasn't thinking straight. It's just that's what I was always taught to do. I feel very responsible for our child. I want to be involved," he said, earnestly. "It all caught me off guard."

Jo smiled and reached across the table to take his hand in hers. His strong hand clasped hers, and it was reassuring.

Warm.

And she couldn't help but think of his hot hands on her skin a month ago. It made her body tingle at the thought of it.

"I really appreciate it. We'll figure this out."

"I'm glad you told me," he said quietly.

"Why wouldn't I?"

"Why should you? I'm just a stranger."

There was a bitter mistrust to his voice, and she wondered who had hurt him so much.

Hurt she understood.

"Well, when I saw you there, and Lloyd told me you were one of the paramedics in town, I figured it would be kind of hard to hide my condition. It'll be there for everyone to see in a few months."

Henrik smiled and rubbed his thumb over her knuckles. Just that simple act made her skin flush and her heart beat a bit faster. She pulled her hand away, quickly.

It may have been a magical night, but it was just one magical night.

That was it.

It was clear that he didn't really want a relationship, and she certainly didn't want to fall in love again. The prospect of falling in love with someone and being hurt was too great. It was too much of a threat to her heart, and she wasn't willing to take that chance.

There was a furious banging at the door.

Henrik got up and answered the back door.

Lloyd came in, his face red. "It's Marge!"

"Marge?" Jo asked.

Lloyd pushed past Henrik. "Marge, one of the local hookers."

"What?" Jo asked, startled.

"She works at the arts emporium. She crochets blankets for the inn and tourists," Henrik explained. "You know…a hooker."

"Lloyd, what's wrong with Marge?" Jo asked, still confused.

"She's in labor, and she's not going to make it to the hospital. She's at the clinic! I came for Henrik, but I'm so glad to see you, Doc Jo!"

"Come on," Henrik said. "I'll take you. Tell Marge and her husband we're on the way, Lloyd."

Lloyd nodded and scurried away.

"It's a busy night," Jo remarked, pulling on her sweater and her boots.

"It's not usually like this, but this is Marge's fifth child. It's no wonder that they're making quite the quick entrance," Henrik said.

They both chuckled at that.

It had been a long time since Jo had attended a

birth. Usually when they came into the emergency room, Obstetrics was called, but she was pretty sure that she could handle this. But tying off a femoral artery in the back of the ambulance didn't jangle her nerves as much as having to attend an emergency birth in her small clinic without the safety net of the hospital. She hoped it was a smooth birth.

It took all of five minutes for them to make it to the center of town and to her small clinic where Lloyd had unlocked the door with a skeleton key and was guiding Marge and her frantic husband, Scott, inside.

Henrik parked on the street, and Jo dashed inside. Jennifer was there looking flustered.

"Oh, thank the Lord," Jennifer said. "I was trying to call an ambulance."

Jennifer looked at Henrik and then at her. Jo tried not to blush.

"Well, I'm here now. Call the ambulance again in case we need it," Jo told her as she made her way over to Marge.

She looked like she was in major pain and was hunched over, Scott holding her up as she panted heavily.

"Doc, I tried to make it to the hospital, but it's coming something fierce," Scott said.

"Let's get her to the exam table so I can check her," Jo said.

Marge cried out, and her water broke all over the waiting-room floor as Henrik stepped inside and locked the door behind him. Marge was sinking to the ground, screaming.

"I don't think she's going to make it to the table, Doc Jo," Henrik remarked. "What do you need?"

"Blankets, gloves… Everything is labeled and ready in the back. Jenn can help."

"Come along, Lloyd," Henrik said, leading a horrified Lloyd out of the waiting room.

Jo tried to lead Marge away from where her water had broken to a cleaner area. Henrik was back with blankets and helped her spread them out. Jo pulled on the rubber gloves that Henrik had brought her. They removed Marge's undergarments, and Jo was glad that Marge was wearing a nightgown. Then she pulled off Marge's rubber boots.

Scott braced his wife's back, behind her.

"I'm going to look now, okay, Marge?" Jo asked.

Marge was biting her lip and nodding.

As soon as Jo checked she could see the head, and internally she was relieved that this appeared to be a run-of-the-mill birth so far, despite the speed. This she could deal with.

"I called Lisa, the midwife for this side of the island, but she's out near Eastern Tickle dealing with an emergency birth there too," Henrik said. "Jennifer said the ambulance is coming."

Marge cried out.

"Well, this baby isn't going to wait for someone to come back from the… Tickle area." Jo shook her head, because she'd never thought that was something she would say in her life. "Marge, when you feel the next contraction, I want you to push. You're crowning."

Marge nodded. "I feel it."

"Then, push for me," Jo urged.

Marge pushed, the head came through, but then it stopped, and Jo's stomach knotted as she mentally tried to flick through her rotation from ages ago when she had been on the obstetrical floor as an intern.

"Okay, Marge. Breathe, no pushing," Jo said, firmly.

"What's wrong?" Henrik asked very quietly, squatting beside her.

"I think it's shoulder dystocia. I've seen it once, but obstetrics wasn't my strong suit," Jo murmured back. She hadn't dealt with it herself, and she was trying to go through the HELPERR guidelines in her head and hoping that she could remember them.

HELPERR was a mnemonic that was used in case of shoulder dystocia and the steps needed to safely deliver the child.

"I've dealt with a birth like this," Henrik said, pulling on gloves. "We can try the McRoberts's maneuver. Then, we'll have to watch for maternal bleeding. I've called the paramedics on duty, but we should see if that procedure will work first."

"McRoberts's is when we pull her legs up and one of us applies pressure, right?" Jo said, as everything came rushing back to her. She smiled up at Henrik, who was being so wonderfully calm and reassuring. She felt like she was the one who was losing control, and he'd centered her in that moment so she could collect her thoughts.

Henrik nodded. "I'll help her hold her legs, and you apply the pressure to make sure the baby's shoulders rotate."

Jo nodded and then raised her voice so her patient could hear. "Marge, I need you to draw your legs up, way up to your stomach. Henrik and Scott will help."

"What's wrong?" Marge asked, wearily.

"Your baby just needs some help. Their shoulder isn't in the optimal position. We're going to try this and see if that helps."

Marge nodded.

Henrik and Scott helped Marge pull up her legs, bracing them as Jo placed one hand on Marge's pelvis, waiting for that next contraction. She glanced up to see Henrik. His gaze fixed on her, and she relaxed. He nodded as if to say she had this. A silent encouragement.

Josephine knew what to do.

This baby would live, as would Marge.

"Marge, when the next contraction comes, push for me," Jo said.

Marge nodded. "It's coming."

Jo felt the tightening of her abdomen as the contraction moved across her. Jo pressed on her suprapubic area, and she could feel the rotation happen. The baby's shoulders slipped free. Jo stopped applying pressure as she caught the baby, who started crying right away at the indignity of being abruptly expelled from her warm home.

"It's girl," Jo announced happily as she cleared away everything, and Henrik wrapped the baby, helping place the crying newborn on Marge's chest. Scott and Marge were already doting on their newest child.

Jo smiled and watched them. She could feel the love, and it warmed her heart. She was also relieved that Henrik had been there to help her. She wasn't sure that she would've handled it so well without him.

The placenta was delivered, and Jo cut the cord. There were no signs of extra bleeding, but Marge and the baby should be taken to the hospital so they could be monitored. As Jo cleaned up and got the placenta placed in a biomedical bag for the obstetrical team to examine, the sound of sirens grew louder until they stopped in front of the clinic.

There were flashing lights illuminating the waiting area.

"I'll go get them," Henrik said, peeling off his rubber gloves and disposing of them.

Jo stood as the team came in, and she gave her instructions and information to the head paramedic so that they could tell the hospital staff what had happened and what to watch for. Henrik assisted in getting Marge settled onto the gurney and the baby into an isolette for safe transport.

"Can I ride with her?" Scott asked.

"There won't be room," Henrik stated. "But I'll take you to the hospital, Scott."

"Ta, thanks, Henrik," Scott said, brightly.

Marge grabbed Josephine's hand, smiling at her. "Thank you for helping me, Doc Jo."

"You're most welcome," Jo said, warmly. "Congratulations! I can't wait to see the little miss for her first checkup in a week."

Marge nodded. "Her name is Josephine. After you."

A lump formed in Jo's throat, and tears stung her eyes. "I'm honored."

Marge let go of Jo's hand as the paramedics wheeled her out of the clinic, with Scott following. She turned to Henrik, who was disposing of the mess.

"Thank you for helping me," Jo said. "I couldn't have done it without you."

Henrik grinned. "I can say the same. I'm glad you were here too."

"I'll check on Lloyd and make sure he gets back home," Jo said, trying not to laugh.

"Oh, good. He was a bit shook up. He may be the voluntary fire chief, but Nubbin's Harbor doesn't usually have this much action."

"I don't know if I can take this much excitement nightly."

Henrik chuckled. "I better take Scott with me. Make sure he gets to the hospital okay. I'll come by tomorrow morning, and we can finish our conversation."

"I think we said all we need to say," Jo said.

"For now." Henrik didn't say anything else and left the clinic.

She didn't know what he meant by that, and she didn't want to overthink it. He was right: they hadn't exactly finished their discussion before Lloyd showed up. She glanced around her waiting room and sighed.

Lloyd peered his head around the corner from her office. "It's safe?"

She smiled. "Yes. You all right to get home?"

Lloyd nodded. "I'll be fine. Tonight calls for a stiff drink. You going to come by and have some more screech?"

Even though tonight did warrant a stiff drink, she was not in a position to indulge, and she didn't feel like explaining the reason to Lloyd. Nubbin's Harbor didn't need to know about her condition quite yet.

"I think I'll pass. I have some cleaning up to do, and I'll have to wait up for a call from the hospital to discuss the birth."

Lloyd quickly ducked his head. "I'll let myself out. Have a good night, Doc Jo."

Lloyd sidestepped the mess and headed out.

Jo breathed a sigh of relief, locked the door to the clinic and then went to look for her cleaning supplies.

Jennifer was filling up a bucket with water. "I thought you'd need this."

"Thanks," Jo said, sighing. "It's been a long day."

"I bet." Jennifer handed her a pair of rubber gloves. "So you've met the Fogo Island heartthrob, eh?"

"Who? Henrik?"

Jennifer grinned. "Aye."

"I met him a month ago."

"And he's the father?"

Jo's eyes widened. "How do you know?"

"I have a kid myself, as well as many sisters, and there's just a look about you."

Jo snorted. "Not the *glow*, surely."

"Also I saw your pregnancy test. You left it on the counter."

Jo groaned. "It's still new. Please don't tell anyone."

"I won't." Jennifer smiled. "I'm happy for you."

Jo shared Jennifer's smile. It was a relief that Jennifer knew, then she wouldn't have to go out of her way to hide it from her. Jennifer was pretty perceptive. "Thanks, Jenn. Now, let's get that waiting room cleaned up!"

Jennifer nodded. "Aye aye, Captain."

Jo took a calming breath. Jennifer had noticed,

and she couldn't help but wonder who else in town would. Who knew a one-night stand could get so complicated?

Henrik had had an out-of-body experience last night when he'd had dinner with Josephine. Of course, last night he'd had a couple. The first was when she'd told him that she was pregnant with his child.

The second had been when he'd suggested they get married. He laughed now thinking of it.

After Melissa had left him standing at the proverbial altar, he'd sworn that he was never going to do that again. He was never going to put his heart on the line like that.

Yet, he just couldn't shake Josephine from his mind. When he'd first seen her on the beach today, he'd reminded himself to keep his distance and keep it professional.

All that came crashing down when she'd told him she was pregnant.

Josephine was already firmly entrenched in his life, and it terrified him. He wasn't sure the walls to his heart were strong enough to resist her or able to handle it when she left. Not if, but when.

She was only here for a year.

Nothing was holding her here.

No ghosts were holding her like they were anchoring him to this island.

He was pretty positive that wherever his gran

was, she was laughing at him for karma coming to kick him in the backside.

After he made sure that Scott was safe at the hospital and reunited with Marge and the wee baby Josephine, he headed back to Nubbin's Harbor. Instead of going straight home, he drove slowly by the clinic and saw that Josephine was mopping the floor. She had her earbuds in, and she was dancing and singing. Her honey-blond hair was in a high ponytail, and periodically she would stop to bang her head and he couldn't help but wonder what type of rock anthem she was listening to.

It was quite the sight. The mother of his child-to-be.

It made him laugh.

She was so adorable and sexy.

And it took all his resolve not to knock on the door of her clinic and join her in her cleaning. Then he caught sight of Jennifer and thought better of it. Though he knew that he should keep his distance from her, there was a part of him that he'd thought was long buried away. A part of his heart that was bucking over the constraints and rules that he'd set for himself.

Didn't his heart know that it was for his own good?

He drove back to his lonely cottage and tried to get a good night's sleep. He was on duty tomorrow afternoon, and he would be driving an ambulance around the island. His first day back to Fogo had been exhausting, so he should have been out as soon as his head hit the pillow. But no matter how much he tried to sleep, he couldn't.

All he could think about was Josephine.

How kind and smart she was. How she made his blood heat and his body ache with need. How much he wanted to get to know her and be around her.

She was consuming him.

Then he thought of their baby and remembered that Josephine was only here for a year and then she'd be moving back to Toronto and taking their child with her, and he felt nauseous.

Even the thought of being a father was thrilling. It was something he'd always wanted but never thought he'd have after Melissa left him.

The chance of a family.

It was like a dream, but he was worried of losing it all when Josephine left.

After hours of tossing and turning he gave up, had a shower and got dressed. With a coffee in hand he decided to take a walk out on the beach, which really was just a collection of smooth flat rocks at the edge of the spit that his defunct lighthouse stood on, but he needed to clear his head and wanted to catch the sunrise over the Atlantic.

As he made his way down toward the shore, out of the corner of his eye he caught sight of a massive iceberg not far off. It was the largest he had seen in some time and made his little cottage look like a tiny speck.

"Wow!" he heard someone gasp.

He rounded a tall rock and found Josephine, in running gear, sitting and staring at the iceberg.

"Good morning," he said, surprised.

She turned, and her eyes widened. "Right, I forgot that this isn't the derelict public beach I thought it was for the last month. I'm sorry."

"It's okay," he said. "I don't mind. I just didn't expect to see you out here."

"I like to run out this way first thing, or rather walk, now I'm pregnant. I like to catch the sunrise." She nodded toward the iceberg. "So this is what the start of iceberg season is like?"

"Yes," he sighed. "I did see a stream of traffic heading toward Joe Batt's Arm and mostly likely Fogo Island Inn for just this."

"I can see why it brings in tourists," she said in awe.

"I'll probably be on some search-and-rescue shifts this week," he said, sitting down next to her on the rocky ledge.

She frowned, pulling down her toque. "I hope not."

"It's inevitable. People want to get up close and personal to the icebergs. I mean, what harm could they really do?"

"You tell me," she said, a smile tugging at the corner of her lips. "This is my first experience seeing them up close."

"Well, they're larger below the water than above."

"Ah, *the tip of the iceberg*, as it were."

He grinned and tapped his nose. "They also can tear out the side of a ship. I'm not just talking about the *Titanic*, but the big cargo vessels from Montreal that bring goods up to northern communities in Labrador and Nunavut. You have to be careful. They're beautiful, but they can be deadly, and we've had one too many close calls."

"Wouldn't the ships just avoid them?"

"They can't always be avoided, and as I said, they're deceptive. Something really small on top could be huge and terrifying underneath. Those ones, you usually find out the damage after the fact."

"Well, I will still try and think positively that nothing too bad will happen."

"This is just the start of the tourist season. Be prepared. It's going to be a busy summer."

"It's not even the end of spring yet," she teased. "And I did deal with a nasty stomach flu that ran through town."

"Exactly."

They shared another smile and then sat in silence staring at the behemoth. It was comfortable just sitting here with her. It felt right, and that was a little bit unnerving. The last time he had been this comfortable with someone had been Melissa, and that had ended in disaster.

"Well, I should get back to the clinic," Josephine announced, standing up. "I have a morning full of appointments. I know you mentioned coming by and talking…"

"Right, well, we can talk another time," he said. "Are you free for dinner again?"

"You have leftovers?" she asked hopefully.

He grinned. "No, I'm having them for my lunch today while on duty. I thought you might like to come to Seldom with me. There's a little place down by the water where we can get something to eat and talk, without so many locals from Nubbin's Harbor milling about."

"I'd like that. I'm not quite ready to tell the world that I'm pregnant."

"Agreed."

That's the last thing he wanted, especially when they still really needed to decide how they planned to coparent this child. They walked back up to the main road.

"What time would you like to meet?" she asked.

"I'll come by your place at six, if that's okay?"

"My last appointment is at four. Six is great."

Josephine put her earbuds back in before waving and slowly walking away. Henrik stood there, admiring her back view, remembering how he had run his hands over those round cheeks.

His blood heated, and his mouth went dry.

Get a grip on yourself.

He shook his head and made his way to his truck. He was going to get some breakfast on the road and try to do something out of town before his afternoon shift started. Something away from Nubbin's Harbor, hoping that old saying *Out of sight, out of mind* would prove true.

Of course, who was he kidding?

He would still be thinking about her. He hadn't stopped thinking about her since he met her.

It hadn't worked when he'd been at sea, and it wouldn't work today. It frustrated him that she was invading his thoughts so completely. That he desired her still, and the strength of his need for her was overruling all the safeguards he'd put into place years ago to protect himself.

What was it about her?

This was not the way to keep someone at bay, and Henrik felt with a sense of looming dread that his defenses were coming down.

CHAPTER FIVE

JO HADN'T PLANNED on seeing Henrik. That was the furthest thing from her mind. All night she had tossed and turned thinking about him, so the last thing she wanted to do was run into him.

After getting barely any sleep she'd decided to go for a light jog, or rather a vigorous walk.

It was something she had picked up when David died. There were so many sleepless nights, so much pent-up anxiety that she took to running as a way to calm herself and face the day.

It was how she started most days on Fogo. She loved the way the mist would creep across the rocks. The calmness of the water and the big blue sky.

There were more uneven roads than the parks in Toronto had, but she didn't mind. It was always a moment of tranquility before other residents woke up.

And she always ended up by the lighthouse. Muscle memory had taken her there without her even thinking about it.

She had to remember it was Henrik's place. If she wanted to keep her distance and maintain a friendly relationship not muddied by her annoying attraction to him, she had to steer clear of him as much as she could.

So the lighthouse was out.

Of course, agreeing to go out to dinner with him wasn't the best idea either.

She was nervous about it, but they had to talk about the baby. Fogo wasn't her permanent home. Toronto was.

Why?

Yes, she'd made a home there with David, but he was gone. Was her job there really so important? She could be a trauma surgeon anywhere. All she knew was that Gary would come back to Nubbin's Harbor within the year, and it was too small for two doctors.

Jo unlocked the back door to the clinic. Jennifer was in the back, prepping the charts for the day.

"How was your run, Jo?"

"I ran into Henrik. I somehow forgot the beach by the lighthouse is his."

"He wouldn't mind," Jennifer said.

"I know. He said as much."

"So I'm curious how you two met," Jennifer said, prying.

"At the pub…my first night. Why?"

Jennifer shrugged. "Henrik is a notorious rake, you know."

Jo cocked an eyebrow. "*Rake?* Isn't that term out of a regency novel or something?"

Jennifer chuckled. "Yes! I love reading historical romance."

Jo grinned. "No judgment. I'm just wondering why you think that Henrik Nielsen is a rake?"

"He's always after the come from aways. Never a local girl." Jennifer paused, clutching the patient charts to her chest. "Actually, I'm surprised he went with you, seeing how you were the new doctor in town and all."

Jo worried her bottom lip. "We never actually talked about that."

Jennifer grinned. "Oh, really? Well, then, it just proves my point. He thought you were a tourist, and he's a rake through and through."

Jo laughed and made her way to her apartment above the clinic to freshen up before the day's patients came in.

Henrik as a rake seemed kind of preposterous, but she knew he didn't pursue the locals, just the come from aways.

And she was one of those.

Does it matter?

The truth was, it didn't. She didn't want another relationship. Still, the idea of Henrik being some kind of firm bachelor only interested in flings was silly.

He didn't seem the type.

He was gentle, kind and witty. There was an air of mischief about him, but it was a fun kind of trouble, and she liked that.

Warmth flooded her cheeks, and she smiled thinking about him and those sparkling blue eyes.

Don't think about him like that.

She groaned, frustrated that she couldn't get him out of her head.

All she and Henrik had to figure out was how they were going to raise this baby and keep their working relationship professional.

Of course today had to be quiet. Which was good for the people of Fogo, but it wasn't good for him. It meant that he'd spent all day thinking about Josephine.

Even his partner Hal's stories which were usually entertaining couldn't keep his mind off his dinner with Josephine or the fact that he had made a complete fool of himself asking her to marry him.

What had he been thinking?

His father had told him to treat women with respect. Always.

And he'd seen it all the time growing up, watching his dad with his mother and his granddad with his gran.

Even though he didn't want a relationship, he never treated his flings badly.

Of course, he never thought he would ever be a father, so he'd thought that the most logical thing to do was get married.

Of course, it was silly.

People didn't have to be married to have a child together. All sorts made up families.

She'd agreed marriage wasn't an option.

He was relieved but also slightly disappointed, and that disappointment worried him. What kind of hold did Josephine have on him? It was completely distracting and frustrating.

He could usually get a one-night stand out of his head immediately, but then they were usually gone the next day and didn't turn out to be the new doctor in town.

A new doctor who was talented and kind. Who was smart, funny and not afraid to get her hands dirty.

People around here trusted her; they liked her. That's what he kept hearing.

She was everywhere on Fogo.

After his uneventful shift, he drove back to his place and had a quick shower, cleaned up and made his way over to the clinic. He was running a bit late, which was unusual for him, but he'd lost track of time thinking about her, and he didn't have Josephine's personal phone number to let her know.

She was outside the clinic, waiting for him.

His pulse kicked up a notch when he pulled up. Even though she was dressed casually in jeans and a nice sweater, with her hair tied back, she still looked stunning.

Just like that first night when he'd looked up from his beer to see her sitting at the other end of the bar. So poised and beautiful. Then their eyes had locked, and it was like he knew her.

He wanted to know her.

He wanted to be with her.

Something had told him that approaching her would be a risk to his heart, but he still had, and for one brief flicker as he reached across the seat to unlock the door, he was glad that he hadn't listened to that warning. She was worth all the distraction.

"I was beginning to worry," she said as she climbed up into the truck. "You're thirty minutes late."

"I'm sorry. I didn't have your number to let you know and I wasn't sure if you would answer the clinic phone line. I know it's for business."

"I was worried you'd hit a moose or a caribou or something."

He glanced over at her and saw the mischievous twinkle in her eyes.

Henrik laughed. "No, just lost track of time."

"So we're off to Seldom. That's near the ferry terminal, isn't it?" she asked.

"Everything is about a twenty-minute drive or so—but, yes, Seldom is down on the other side of the island. There's a great little place by the shore that has the best lobster and crab. Or, if you're more adventurous, sea cucumber."

Josephine wrinkled her nose and looked slightly horrified. "Sea cucumbers, aren't they those slimy things?"

"They're echinoderms. Marine invertebrates. Sea urchins are the hard, spiky version, and sea cucumbers are soft."

Why are you talking about marine animals, b'y?
Now he was the one rambling.

"People eat them?"

"Yes. Although, mostly our sea-cucumber harvest is used in pharmaceuticals. Like collagen powder and...other medicines." He cleared his throat, hoping that he wasn't blushing and that she understood what he meant.

"What other medicines?" she asked, carefully.

"Herbal remedies."

"You mean for men?" she asked, cocking an eyebrow. There was a wicked smile on her face.

"Well..."

"Why are you so familiar with the herbal remedies?" she teased.

"I'm informed," he said, pretending his pride was wounded.

"I see. Good to know. Perhaps it's something I can prescribe, since it's all-natural."

Henrik groaned. "I don't want to know. This is a strange conversation."

"You started it."

He chuckled. "I suppose I did."

It was so easy to have a laugh with her. It was so easy to talk to her about the oddities and facts he'd picked up over the years and she wasn't grossed out by the conversation. He could never talk to Melissa like this and certainly not the women that came before Josephine.

"I'm a doctor. I'm familiar with certain medicines. I just didn't know sea cucumbers were involved."

"Well, now you know."

"How about we stick to lobster?" Josephine suggested. "Besides, lobster is safe for me to eat. Echinoderms, probably not."

"Right. I didn't even think of that."

"Lobster is fine," she affirmed.

"Is there anything that's particularly bothering you? I forgot to ask."

"Are you asking if I have morning sickness?" she asked, gently.

He nodded. "I remember your aversion to fish after you kissed the cod."

Josephine laughed, and he liked the way she did it with her whole body. "Right. Well, maybe I'll pass on the cod too. Only if it's cold and floppy. Maybe if the fishy smell is overpowering it might trigger something, but honestly I haven't had much morning sickness yet. A bit of food aversion and nausea, just sometimes."

"That's good."

An awkward silence fell between them, and he didn't know what else to talk about. He didn't know what to ask her.

He was going to be a father, and he felt absolutely useless.

"I have a dating ultrasound appointment on Monday at the hospital. You're welcome to attend," she said, breaking the silence.

He was surprised. "You want me there?"

"I'm offering you the chance to be there if you want to. You still seem a little bit blindsided about the whole thing."

"I am a bit."

"Didn't you ever want a family?" she asked.

"A long time ago," he said, softly.

"What changed?"

He shrugged, not wanting to talk about his pain or loss. "Just never met the right person."

"So you're okay with this?" she asked, carefully.

He smiled at her. "I am. I just didn't think... I didn't expect this."

"Same," she muttered. "I'm thirty-eight, and this might be my last chance."

He cocked an eyebrow. "You're thirty-eight?"

"Yes," she said, cautiously. "How old are you?"

"Thirty-one. Or I will be next month."

Now it was her turn to be a bit shocked. Her mouth dropped open, and her eyes widened. "I didn't realize you were so much younger than me."

"I thought you were my age or younger, but if you're a trauma surgeon who's been at it a while, there was a part of me that was wondering if you had been some kind of child prodigy."

Josephine laughed again. "No, not a child prodigy. I always had good grades, but I did it all on the regular timeline."

"I'm surprised you're still single," he said. "A

woman like you, so beautiful and warm, you should've been snapped up a long time ago."

Her expression softened. "I wasn't always single. I was married."

"What happened?" he asked, gently.

"He died three years ago."

Jo wasn't exactly expecting to talk about David tonight, but Henrik was the father of her child, and it was important that they get to know each other. When Henrik had just been a one-night stand, their ages hadn't matter. She knew he was over twenty-five by the few errant strands of gray. And it certainly didn't matter about their past romantic history. Henrik hadn't needed to know about David then.

Now it was different, and there was no point in keeping it all secret.

Henrik had the right to know that she had been married once, but he didn't need to know about how much it had damaged her heart and how she still felt raw inside three years later. She didn't have to tell him all that.

That was her pain to bear. Not his.

She didn't like to talk about it. It had been bad enough her friends and family always seemed to want to. So she steered clear of the subject with new people, but Henrik deserved to know.

Even though it hurt.

What she didn't want was secrets from each other.

Not if they were going to make this coparenting thing work.

They had to be friends.

They had to trust each other and be a united, platonic front to raise their baby.

"I'm sorry," Henrik said, gently shaking her from her thoughts. "Grief is…complicated."

And she got the sense that he knew, but she didn't press him.

She understood it was hard to talk about it sometimes.

"It is," she said, wistfully.

"May I ask how?"

"Aneurysm. We went to bed one night after a long shift, and when I woke up the next morning he was gone. He had passed away beside me in the night, in his sleep." She tried to swallow the lump that formed in her throat every time she talked about David.

"Is that why you left Toronto?" he asked.

"No. I told you, I'm helping out a friend."

Liar.

Yes, she was helping out her friend, but she was also running away from the memories. Running away from the hospital where they'd both worked and had been happy. She was running away from the pain, because everywhere she went in that hospital she only saw him.

She felt him.

And if she was going to ever move on with her life, she needed a change, and Fogo was it.

For now.

"Right, I forgot. Well, I'm sorry. I didn't mean to bring up such a touchy subject."

"It's okay. I want you to know. We're going to have a baby together, and I would like us to be friends as we coparent, if that's what you want?"

"I told you. I'm all in."

Her heart skipped a beat. She was happy he was all in. It gave her hope this could work. "Good. I'm glad."

They drove through the town of Seldom. It reminded her of Nubbin's Harbor, just a bit larger. It had the same kind of brightly colored houses.

Seldom had a bigger wharf area and ships out in the water. This is where they farmed the sea cucumbers, lobster and other marine life in their fishing cooperative. Henrik drove down to a little shanty that was by the shore. It looked busy, and there were a lot of cars full of tourists that were coming off the ferry. She hoped they would be able to get a table. She was starving, and she had her tasters set to a nice lobster dinner with melted butter and potatoes.

Her stomach growled at the thought.

Was this going to be her life now? Letting her stomach rule her thoughts and actions? She smiled to herself. It was a small price to pay to have something she always wanted. When she and David had begun to try for a baby, they'd had such a hard time, and in the end David hadn't wanted her to continue with the treatments.

It still seemed kind of shocking to her that this time, with Henrik, even using contraception she'd conceived.

Almost like a miracle.

She'd heard of pregnancy miracles before. Read about them, tried to figure out how the miracle worked and then never quite believed it.

Until now.

And she was ever so thankful.

"Looks a bit busy tonight," Henrik remarked.

"I hope we can get a table," Jo agreed.

"We will," he said with confidence. "I called ahead."

"That was smart."

"It's the start of iceberg season. I know that Newfoundland doesn't seem like much of a tourist hot spot compared to the rest of the world, but it is. It's a beautiful place, and one I'm happy to call home."

"I don't doubt it," Jo said quietly. "I hope you know I wasn't disparaging your home."

He grinned. "I know, but we're going to have to get used to tourists invading our space soon."

"I think I can deal with that. Toronto was wall-to-wall people on the regular."

They got out of Henrik's truck and headed into the little restaurant. It was busy, but there was a table waiting for them by the big bay window that looked out over the harbor of Seldom.

The waitress approached them with menus. "Our specials tonight are cod and rock lobster."

Jo cringed at the thought of cod, and when she glanced up at Henrik he was smirking, his blue eyes twinkling at her.

"I think we'll both have the rock lobster," Henrik said. "I'll have an iced tea."

The waitress nodded and wrote it down and then she looked at Jo. "And what will you have, ducky?"

"Iced tea sounds great, and maybe a glass of water."

The waitress smiled and took their menus, before scurrying off.

"I will never get used to that term of endearment."

Henrik chuckled. "It does take some getting used to. Is there any other slang you're not used to? Something I can clear up?"

"Hmm, well I've been referred to as *saucy*, and I didn't think that I was being sarcastic at the time."

A dimple popped in his cheek. "Let me guess. Lloyd?"

"Yes. He said, 'She's some saucy, b'y.' And I'm not sure that I should take that as a compliment."

"You can in Lloyd's case," Henrik said. "He means you're clever. You're quick on your feet. Lloyd likes you. I mean you did kiss the cod on your first night in Nubbin's Harbor. You didn't shy away from it. You've got gumption, and Lloyd likes that."

Josephine wrinkled her nose thinking about the cod again. "And that's why I'm having lobster tonight instead of cod."

They both laughed at that.

"So about the baby…" Henrik said.

"Yes. We have to figure out a way to do this."

"Agreed. We're going to have to work together."

"Right. I want to keep things professional," Josephine said, firmly.

"As do I. We're both adults. We can do this."

"Yes. We can."

Jo had to make this work. She didn't want to deny Henrik his child, but she also didn't want to fall in love with someone again, and certainly not someone who had no interest in a relationship. Although, the more she got to know Henrik, the more she could see herself being with a man like him.

He's off-limits.

Still, it was hard not to think of him like that. Not when he made her pulse race and she recalled his delicious kisses.

She wanted to be around him, but it was hard to keep up the protective walls around her heart when she was. "So are there any other questions?" Henrik asked. "About Fogo, that is."

She grinned. "Maybe some more language stuff."

"Shoot," Henrik said, confidently.

"Okay, so bayfolk are people who live around the bay, and townies are those from St. John's, and come from aways are tourists."

"Yes, b'y!" He winked.

"Nar bit?"

"Nothing left," Henrik stated.

"Well, I think by the year's end, I should have it all down pat."

"I've heard there's some discussion about pronunciation of the word *Toronto*."

"Well, if you're from Toronto, and indeed a certain part of Toronto, you pronounce it as *Tahrahna* rather than *Toerontoe*."

Henrik's eyebrows rose. "Interesting."

"People in different parts of Ontario have different accents too."

"I'll have to go to Ontario one time. Maybe."

"You've never been?" Josephine asked.

"Never been much of anywhere," Henrik said, offhandedly. "I did some schooling in Halifax, but I've never left the Maritimes...other than going north to Nunavut."

"Well, I hope you can get to see more of the world one day."

His spine stiffened. "I'm not one for traveling. Why would I? This is my home."

It was the way he said that this was his home, like she had insulted him or something. And she couldn't help but wonder what had got his back up. She knew there were people who were so attached to their homes and didn't want to travel far from the place of their birth, but he did seem to have a curiosity about other places. So why did he become closed off when she mentioned traveling?

Don't worry about it. It's not your problem.

Only, it was her problem. She wasn't going to settle here in Newfoundland; at least, that wasn't the plan, and if he wanted to be in their child's life, then he was going to have to travel to Ontario to spend time with their kid. She couldn't always be coming to Newfoundland.

And she couldn't stay.

Even if she was really starting to enjoy her life here.

Gary would come home from Germany, and she wouldn't have a job.

Her sabbatical from the hospital was only a year, and she couldn't see herself giving up her life, her work as a trauma surgeon in Toronto, for anything.

Couldn't you?

Toronto had been a place she'd loved as a child and the city she and David had made their home, but other than her job, there were no ties there. David was gone; her grandparents were gone. Her parents weren't there. Toronto was familiar, but nothing was holding her there.

She could work anywhere, and she had a feeling her mother would want her to come to Arizona, but she had no desire to leave Canada.

Still, how could she leave Toronto and the memories there?

She wasn't sure that she could or that it would be right. It felt a bit like a betrayal.

David would want you to be happy.

Yet, there was a part of her that told her Fogo could become home, even if she was scared to admit it.

Henrik didn't mean to close himself off to her when she'd suggested that he travel. It was just a bit of a defense mechanism that he couldn't seem to stop. Melissa had always talked about leaving Newfoundland and moving back out west. She'd been obsessed with the West, and he'd always told her that he didn't want to go. Melissa told him it was okay and that she loved him, and he'd foolishly believed that. He'd believed he was enough.

Until she'd left him for the West, and he just couldn't follow.

This was his home.

It was the place his parents lived, and they were who knit him. Family who lived here for generations, and he wasn't about to leave. He couldn't leave: this place was in his blood.

"Remember where you're from," his dad had told him as they walked along the beach.

"I will, Da," Henrik had said. "I wish I could come with you and Mum."

His da had smiled down at him, squatting next to him to look him in the eyes.

"Not this time. You can stay with Gran and your mum, and I will be back before you know it. You can watch for us from here in two days."

"Promise?" Henrik had asked.

"Aye. No worry… We'll come back. Just wait for us."

And that's what he'd done. Fogo was the place his family loved.

The place he loved. He couldn't have betrayed his family or left his gran all alone like that.

Of course, he'd thought it was in Melissa's blood too, but it wasn't, and it wasn't in Josephine's blood either, and it probably wouldn't be in his child's unless he could convince Josephine that Newfoundland and Fogo Island was a great place to call home and raise a child.

He had always been happy here, even after losing his parents.

So even though marriage was off the table for him and Josephine, he could work hard to convince her to stay put so they could raise their child together. Couldn't he?

He at least wanted to try. He just had to show her the very best of it, which in his opinion wouldn't be that hard at all.

The waitress brought their dinners.

"Here you are, duckies," the waitress said, cheerily. "Enjoy! And I just got word there's swiles out in the harbor!"

"Ta," Henrik said as the waitress left.

Josephine cocked a finely arched brow. *"Swiles?"*

"Seals."

"Oh, really?" she asked, excitedly.

"Most likely. Have you never seen a seal in the wild before?"

"No, never. There are no wild seals in southern Ontario."

"Well, we'll take a walk down and see if we can spy them."

"I would like that."

Henrik passed her the butter, without her having to ask. "What do you think of Fogo and Newfoundland so far?"

He wanted to know, so he could figure out what he needed to do to show her the very best of it all.

"I like it," she said, taking the butter from him. "I haven't seen much, though. When I landed in St. John's, it was sunny and beautiful. Driving here was rainy and foggy…"

"Mauzey," he suggested, winking.

"I feel like I'm learning another language here," she teased.

"Sorry, go on," he urged.

"It was rainy and *mauzey.* I was tired and had just got into a car that I had bought online before I landed and headed here. I didn't see much, although I did see some caribou."

"Where?" he asked.

"Swimming alongside the ferry!"

Henrik chuckled. "That's not uncommon."

"It really feels like I'm at the very edge of the known world here."

"But do you like it so far?"

She cocked her head to one side. "So many questions."

"Usually the women I meet are passing through and are here to see specific things, so I'm curious what brings a big-city girl like you here."

A blush tinged her cheeks. "A change, but I am enjoying it here. I would like to see more before I leave. I would like to really get to know Newfoundland before I head back to Ontario."

"We can arrange that."

And he smiled to himself as they ate their dinner. She wanted to know Newfoundland before she returned home, but his plan was that she would get to know Newfoundland so well she wouldn't want to go back to Ontario.

And then she'd become a bayman or townie after all.

CHAPTER SIX

AFTER DINNER THEY made their way down to the shore so that Josephine could see the seals in the water. He was hoping they would still be there when they got down to the pier, and sure enough, they were.

They were barking and swimming in the water.

"This is amazing," Josephine whispered.

"Aye. It is," he admitted. He didn't often take the time to admire the seals. It was just something he took for granted as a local. Josephine took a step but teetered on the uneven path. He reached out and steadied her.

"Thanks," she said. "I keep forgetting how rocky some of these paths are here."

Henrik held her close for a moment. She felt so small, so warm in his arms. He could catch the scent of vanilla in her hair.

And he remembered running his hands through her silken tresses.

Henrik took a step back quickly.

Josephine had a flush to her cheeks.

"You're welcome. If you think this is bad, check out the fjords near Gros Morne on the main island."

"I would like to see them one day," she said, a nervous lilt to her voice.

"I think we can make that work."

He hadn't wanted to let her go, but what reason did he have to hold onto her? Josephine headed down the path in front of him so she could take some pictures of the seals.

Josephine snapped a couple, and they continued walking along the water until he spied a shed that was all lit up, with fiddle music wafting out. It was a public party that had just started up.

Shed parties were fun and full of island life and friendliness.

If he wanted to get Josephine to fall in love with Fogo, this was a great start.

"Come on," he said, taking her delicate hand in his.

"Where are we going?" she asked, following him.

"To a shed party."

She stopped. "Are we invited?"

Henrik chuckled. "It's not like that. This is a public one. It's put on for tourists, and even though you're technically not one, you're still not from here, and I think that everyone should experience a proper shed party once in their life."

Josephine worried her bottom lip. "As long as I don't have to kiss anything."

"I promise, no kissing cod or anything else." Although, in that moment, holding her hand along the shore he didn't really want to make that promise to her. Not when kissing her was something he wanted to do badly. Even though he couldn't.

They'd both agreed to keep their relationship platonic and professional.

Thinking about kissing her was wrong. Remembering the softness of her lips was bad.

He shouldn't think like that because he couldn't have her. He couldn't kiss her.

He wanted to.

He could still remember the way her lips had felt under his.

Vividly.

It made his blood heat, and it was taking all his willpower not to do that. If he was romancing a tourist, this would be a perfect moment.

Only, Josephine was not a regular hookup.

She was far more dangerous to his heart.

They climbed the rocky path up to the shed. The music was loud, and there was singing and laughter through the open windows.

The man at the entrance was selling tickets. "Yes, b'y, I can sell you two tickets. The money is going back into the township to fund grants for the arts."

"Let me buy the tickets," Josephine said, pulling out a ten-dollar bill. "You paid for dinner, Henrik. It's the least I can do."

The man smiled and handed over the ticket stubs. "There will be a raffle later on."

Henrik nodded, and they walked into the crowded shed. The plywood walls were lined with pictures and postcards. There was a map drawn on the wall full of colored thumbtacks that marked where the come from aways were from.

"You have to mark your hometown," Henrik said, fishing out a pink pin.

Josephine smiled and took the tack from him and marked Goderich, Ontario. The first pin in that location.

"Hey," a voice that sounded vaguely familiar said behind them. "I worked for a spell in London, Ontario, and did some work in Goderich!"

Henrik and Jo turned around, and his eyes flew open wide as his gaze landed on someone he hadn't seen in close to five years.

"George Aklavik!"

"Rik!" George opened his arms, and they embraced. "I knew you were from Fogo, but I honestly didn't think I would run into you. This was a last-minute trip, and I thought you'd be out with the coast guard or too busy for me."

Henrik grinned. "G'wan with cha, b'y. Never too busy for the likes of you."

They hugged again, and then he turned to Josephine who was smiling but looked a bit stunned at their greeting.

"Dr. Josephine York, this is one of my oldest friends, George Aklavik, from Cape Recluse in Nunavut."

Josephine's eyes widened. "Cape Recluse? How did you two meet?"

George was grinning that big smile that endeared

him to everyone who knew him. "Henrik did some training missions up there. Our doctor, Dr. James, insisted on it when I was starting out as an air paramedic, and he was just a brand-new coast guard and first responder doing ice rescues."

"It was bloody cold," Henrik recalled.

"It still is!" They all laughed at that.

"I never thought I would see you in Fogo," Henrik said as they found a small corner to sit down together.

"I was flying bush planes in Northern Ontario for a few years with my wife, Samantha. Then we moved to Iqaluit to work and bring up our kids."

"You're married?" Henrik asked, surprised.

"Yep. For a few years now. She's a pilot paramedic as well."

"I'm happy for you," Henrik said.

"What about you?" George asked.

"No, not married."

George glanced at Josephine. "I'm sorry for hogging the conversation. So you're from Goderich, Ontario? What brought you to Fogo?"

"Work," Josephine said. "Covering for a friend. I'm a trauma surgeon in Toronto."

George looked impressed. "A trauma surgeon. Impressive. If you're looking for work after your time is up in Fogo, we're always looking for surgeons in Iqaluit. My brother-in-law is a neonatal surgeon there."

"Now I'm impressed," Josephine said, with awe. "You have a neonatal surgeon up there?"

"My sister was too much of a pull for him," George teased, winking.

"How long are you in Fogo for?" Henrik asked.

"For a couple of days, then I head back up north. My wife is due with our third child, and she'll be very angry if I miss it." George finished off his ale. "I'll be back in a moment," he said and made his way through the crowd.

"He seems friendly," Josephine said. "It almost makes me want to check out Iqaluit to work, if I didn't loathe winter so much."

"You're Canadian, ducky. You're supposed to be used to winter," Henrik teased.

"I'm used to it. Doesn't mean I like it," she murmured.

George came back with three pints of ale, which Henrik knew that Josephine couldn't drink, but it was very generous of George.

"Sorry, if you don't like the brew, I can get you something else," George said.

"I like it," Josephine said, quickly. "I just can't drink it at the moment."

There was a deep blush in her cheeks, and it took George about three seconds to put it all together.

"Oh! Would you like an iced tea or a pop instead?" George asked.

"I'll get it," Henrik said, clapping George on the back.

He disappeared into the crowd, looking back once to see that Josephine and George were leaning over the table to talk. The fiddle music was getting louder, and someone brought out a drum.

It was at that moment that a reel began. Henrik was stuck on one side of the shed and Josephine was on the other, but he wasn't worried about George saying anything that he wouldn't want Josephine to know. George didn't know about Melissa.

The only people that knew were the original folks of Nubbin's Harbor. The ones that knew he had been stood up when Melissa had left the island to go back to Vancouver. Even then, they kept that to themselves and didn't trouble him with it.

There was a part of him that wanted to tell Josephine about Melissa, but he also didn't want to burden her with problems that were private. Although, perhaps it would be best if he told her. She had told him about her late husband. Josephine understood grief. She understood pain and a broken heart.

If anyone was a safe person to talk to it would be her, but he just couldn't at the moment.

"You're too closed off, Henrik," Melissa had said over the phone.

"What're you talking about?" he'd said.

"You never tell me anything. You keep everything close to your chest. You don't want to talk about our future, you just want to stay in one place and raise kids. That's all I know. Do you even feel anything? You're so stoic and serious."

"I have laughs."

"That's not what I mean, and you know it. What're you afraid of, Henrik?"

He shook it away. He didn't need those memories to invade his head. They should be gone, buried. Just like his heart.

Just like his parents.

Of course, they were just empty graves in the Nubbin's Harbor cemetery. Only the sea knew where his parents really were. How many days had he waited out there on the beach, the last place he had seen them?

Yet they were still lost.

He took a deep breath and headed outside of the shed to get some fresh air. It was all suddenly a little stifling. He walked a few paces away from the party and the light and stared up at the clear sky. There was no moon, but the inky black of the sky was painted full of stars that reflected onto the rippling, churning waters of the Atlantic.

He could never leave this place.

This was the only thing that held his heart. However, he knew deep down that despite all his efforts to persuade her to stay, Josephine would leave with their baby. Fogo wasn't her home.

She didn't have ghosts or tragic memories holding her back.

Why let them hold you back, then?

"Hey," Josephine said, coming up behind him. "You left."

"I needed some air, and the dancing was a little much." Henrik reached down, without thinking and took Josephine's hand. Even though he knew he shouldn't, he wanted that moment of human contact. Even if only for a moment. It felt so right to hold her hand. It scared him. He swallowed down his emotions. "Come on. I promised you an iced tea."

Jo had never been one to enjoy herself at parties. David had liked them, because he was definitely more social that she was. And even though she spent her time in very loud and crowded emergency rooms, it was the quiet of the operating room that calmed her.

She was an introvert at heart and didn't mind sticking to David like glue when they were out, so this was a new experience, this shed party in Seldom. Another way to break out of her shell. When David died she'd isolated herself so much.

It was loud, and there was music and dancing, lots of laughing and a great mix of bayfolk, townies and come from aways, as the locals put it, but this was the first time in a long time that she was enjoying herself.

And she actually liked being a part of it all. It made her feel like she wasn't completely alone.

She felt like she belonged.

Henrik's friend George and some of the locals had made her so welcome. They were friendly, and she didn't feel awkward or like she had to make a lot of banal small talk that would frustrate her to no end.

She wasn't that square peg trying to fit in a round hole like she thought she'd be when she first came here.

It was like she fit in perfectly with the people of Fogo.

Henrik had been drafted to take over for the resident fiddler, and she had been shocked when he took the instrument and placed it under his chin and began to play a sea shanty with ease. She couldn't help but tap her foot and clap her hands in time with the music.

He looked over the bow and fiddle and winked at her, his eyes lit up, and she could feel warmth flood her cheeks, her heart beating a bit faster as their gaze locked over the crowd of people.

You're supposed to be keeping your distance with him. You're supposed to be platonic.

She'd agreed to come to dinner tonight because she thought they were going to talk about the baby and their plans about coparenting, except they'd barely talked about that at all. They'd fallen into other conversations, and what was a bit unnerving was that it was so easy to do that with Henrik Nielsen.

So easy.

It was comfortable. Just like when he reached out and took her hand, and she didn't pull away because it felt so good. It felt right.

It calmed her.

And the last time this had happened to her was when she'd met David. The fact that Henrik was making her feel like this made her nervous. She was trying to convince herself that she was falling into this trap too easily, because Henrik himself had admitted that he'd often sleep with women that were just passing through.

Only, she wasn't passing through. She was living here.

For now, a little voice reminded her.

Suddenly, she didn't feel as comfortable in this crowd of people, and she told George that she needed a breath of fresh air. Her stomach was churning. Maybe morning sickness was starting to kick in.

Right now she felt dizzy and out of sorts, and it felt like the walls of the shed were closing in on her. She found her way outside and stood there, taking in deep breaths of air. The music stopped, and there was cheering and some talking.

She turned as more people filtered outside, and she saw Henrik come outside, his hands in his pockets.

"You didn't have to stop," she said. "I just needed some fresh air. I was feeling a bit nauseous."

"I hope it wasn't my fiddle playing?" he teased.

She laughed. "No, it's being crammed in with a lot of people, and it was getting a bit stuffy in there."

Plus she was worried about her end date on Fogo. She was worried about the baby and Henrik being separated for long periods of time. The only thing she was certain of was that the baby wasn't a mistake.

They could make it work for the baby.

Couldn't they?

"The shed party is ending. I said goodnight to George. I'll see him tomorrow before he flies off in the evening," Henrik said. "How about I get you back home?"

"Yes. I think I've had enough excitement tonight. Lobster, swiles and a shed party."

"And that's just the tip of the iceberg!"

Jo rolled her eyes. "That's such a bad pun."

Henrik grinned and took her hand. Though she should pull away, she didn't. The path was rocky back to where his truck was parked, and she really didn't want to trip in the darkness.

"Sorry we didn't get to talking about the baby much," he said, reading her mind. "That was my original intention, I swear."

"Mine too. We still have to talk about that. We

have to make plans other than our agreement to be professional."

"I know. And I mean what I say. I want to be involved with the baby and your pregnancy. I'll do whatever I can." He reached down and touched her face, his knuckles brushing gently against her cheeks.

It made her week in the knees, his touch sending a rush through her, making it harder to breathe.

She looked up at him. "I really appreciate that."

"I care about you."

"You only just met me," she said, softly.

"There are some people you meet and you just know. It's easy."

She understood that too well. She had felt that way with David, and she felt that way with Henrik too. It was usually so hard for her to be intimate or close to anyone unless she felt some kind of connection that was difficult to put into words.

Her skin heated, and she was glad that it was dark and he couldn't see her blushing, but she shivered and Henrik pulled her closer.

"I understand that," she whispered, her voice breaking as she leaned in to the warmth of his body.

"I think… I think I'm going to make a big mistake," he murmured against her ear.

"Oh?"

"Aye." He leaned down and kissed her. The moment his lips touched her, all those internal arguments she was having with herself seemed to melt away into a big puddle of goo. Jo became lost in the sensation of his lips, the touch of his hands cupping her face and the heat of his body pressed against hers.

Henrik made her feel alive.

He made her feel safe too, something she hadn't felt in a long time.

This was bad.

This was not what she wanted, even though there was a part of her that really did and was enjoying it. It was what she had been thinking about for the last month. His mouth on her again. She wanted to be in his arms, melting into him. But wasn't that what had got her into her current predicament?

Pregnant.

She broke off the kiss, even though she didn't want to do that. It was for the best, for her heart's sake. "I can't."

Henrik swallowed. "I'm sorry."

"It's okay. I wanted it too, but…we agreed on a professional relationship."

"I know." He cleared his throat and took a step back from her. "Come on, let's get you home."

Jo nodded.

They headed back to his truck. Not saying much, and the awkward tension was more than she could bear. What she needed was a couple of days away from him to process what was happening, and then maybe they could talk about the baby and set some boundaries.

Boundaries were very important.

There was a time frame to her life here on Fogo Island, and because of that, there could be nothing between them.

Except their child.

CHAPTER SEVEN

AFTER HENRIK HAD dropped Josephine off, he went home, where he tossed and turned all night again. He was unable to get that kiss out of his mind. He wasn't sure what had come over him in that moment.

Especially after they'd agreed to be platonic.

That had lasted all of—what?—five minutes?

He had watched her when he'd been playing music. Actually, he couldn't take his eyes off her all night. She was enchanting, glowing as she smiled and laughed with George and the other locals as well as the other come from aways that had stopped in for the charity shed party.

He loved the way she laughed, the way her eyes lit up and her kindness shone for everyone around her to see. It was like she belonged here.

It was like she was a part of Fogo already, and she'd only been here for a little over a month.

It strengthened his resolve to convince her to stay, so the baby could be in his life on a regular basis. He didn't relish being parted by a long distance from his child.

He was tired of everyone leaving him.

So when he'd found her outside because she needed some air, he couldn't help himself, holding her so close she overwhelmed his senses, and he was pulled inexorably into kissing her again. He was very familiar with the taste of her kisses and the softness of her lips.

It was even better than he remembered.

When she pushed him away, he came to his senses. He didn't want to fall in love. Having her remain on Fogo or in Newfoundland was one thing so he could see his child, but falling in love with Josephine was not acceptable.

His heart was in danger.

After giving up on sleep, he had a cold shower and headed out for his shift, and then he was going to see George at the hotel where those on the training course were staying. It was better that he didn't see Josephine for the next couple of days.

Even driving past her clinic on the main road toward the hospital made his pulse kick up a notch and his palms sweaty.

Suddenly he felt like a young man with his first crush, and he didn't like that feeling at all. He had worked so hard to protect his heart, he didn't expect to feel this out of control.

He changed in the locker rooms into his paramedic uniform and met his partner outside.

"Should be a quiet day," Hal said cheerily. "Although, it's a bit mauzey out."

"Oh, me nerves, b'y. You know you've just jinxed us," Henrik teased.

Hal was fairly new, and he cocked an eyebrow. "How do you mean?"

"It's foggy and you never, ever say it's going to be a quiet day," Henrik stated.

"G'wan with cha. This is the best kind of day!" Hal scoffed.

"How do you figure that?" Henrik asked.

"No one is going to be driving out in mauzey weather," Hal insisted.

"And why do you assume that?"

"Think, man!" Hal tapped his head. "Would you be out sightseeing on a day like this?"

"No, I can't say that I would."

"See. Should be quiet," Hal said, beaming.

Henrik just chuckled. "You better hope so."

Henrik sat down on the bumper of the ambulance and sipped his strong coffee slowly. He was tired and felt groggy. This was not how he liked to start a day. He took his work very seriously. He usually ate healthily and went to bed early.

All that had changed since he'd got back and had found that the new doctor in town was the most tempting woman he'd seen in a long time.

Henrik shook his head, trying not to groan out loud.

"Hey!"

Henrik looked up to see George heading over to him, grinning.

"What're you doing here?" Henrik asked.

"Training got canceled for the day. The instructor is stuck in Farewell. Too foggy out for a ferry run. So I thought I'd come and lend a hand with you today. I got the okay from Health Services."

"You mean it's too mauzey out," Hal corrected, winking.

George laughed, and Henrik just sighed. "Ignore him. Well, I'll be glad to have your help, but it's not all that exciting."

"It's more exciting than walking around town. Which I have done," George said. "Twice."

"I wouldn't count on excitement," Henrik said, and the moment he said that, Hal got a call on the radio.

"Accident near Tilting. Multiple cars. Lots of casualties," Hal stated, grimly.

Henrik looked at George. "Let's go."

George nodded, and they climbed into the rig. Hal hopped into the driver's seat and flicked on the siren and flashing lights.

They crossed the island in record time, not that it took too long to cross it normally. The closer they got to Tilting, the foggier it was, and soon he could see the caution lights from the RCMP on the road and emergency crew.

The RCMP directed the ambulance through the road-closure signs to where there were about six cars that had collided with a truck.

"The most wounded is with the doctor who was on call. Most of the other injuries are superficial, according to the doctor," the police officer said.

Hal pulled the ambulance over to where the doctor was kneeling on the ground by a patient. A totaled car was nearby.

George helped Henrik get the stretcher down, and they wheeled it over to where the doctor was. As they got closer, he saw it was Josephine. She was in scrubs.

She glanced over her shoulder, and her eyes widened only for a moment when she saw him. "I suspect the patient has a broken clavicle and possibly a broken neck. We're going to need a backboard and a halo."

"A broken neck?" Henrik asked, in shock.

Josephine's lips pressed together in a firm line. "The air ambulance can't get through the fog, but if we can stabilize him and get him to the hospital, then hopefully it will give this fog time to clear."

George nodded. "I'll take a first-aid kit and tend to the other wounded."

"Thanks, George," Josephine said, turning back to the patient.

Hal retrieved a halo, and Henrik knelt down on the other side of the patient. He was surprised at how alert the man was.

"This is silly," the man groaned. "I'm just here to see the icebergs."

"What's your name?" Henrik asked, trying to keep the man occupied as Josephine continued her examination of him.

"Saul," the injured man replied. "I'm from Edmonton."

"Edmonton is a distance," Henrik commented as he got ready to set up an intravenous line so they could administer pain meds and antibiotics. Placing someone in a halo brace in the field wasn't exactly the most pleasant thing in the world.

"Yeah, I lived there my whole life, and I never seen the ocean. Never traveled… This was supposed to be a once-in-a-lifetime trip." Saul snorted. "Some trip."

"Saul," Josephine said, interrupting. "We're going to be attaching a halo to keep your neck from moving so we can transport you. It's very important you stay still."

Saul looked nervous.

Josephine took the halo from Hal, who sat at Saul's head. The three of them worked together to make sure that there was no undue movement to the patient. A broken neck could go bad fast, and they needed to make sure that everything was secure so they could get him to the hospital.

Henrik had placed halos before.

Usually, though, the patients weren't this alert.

Saul seemed calm, and Henrik wondered if the patient could move at all or if the spinal cord been severed.

Josephine was calm as she got the halo on.

"Okay, we're going to slowly get you on the backboard and then take you to the hospital," she said.

An RCMP officer came over. "All air transport has been suspended, but the ferry is cleared."

"This man needs to get to a trauma center," she stated.

"We can take the ambulance," Henrik said. "St. John's is three hours going at the speed limit. So we'll get there faster, especially with an escort."

"I can escort you," the officer said.

Josephine nodded. "And I'll go, but I need someone to stay behind here to be with the wounded."

"I'll stay," George said, coming over. "As long as one of these officers can take me back to Fogo proper later on. I can treat everyone else."

The RCMP officer nodded. "No worries, someone will take care of you."

"Then, that's what we'll do," Josephine said, firmly. "Saul, were you alone or was someone traveling with you?"

"My wife is at the Fogo Island Inn," Saul said.

"I'll make sure she's notified, and one of my officers will bring her to St. John's," the RCMP officer said before walking off to speak to the other Mounties.

They finished securing Saul, then Henrik and Hal raised the gurney and Josephine carried the IV bag as they made their way to the back of the ambulance. They loaded Saul in and secured him. Josephine secured the IV line and then sat down in the back.

Hal got into the driver's seat, and Henrik climbed into the back to assist Josephine.

The RCMP officer that was escorting them got into his cruiser and turned on his lights, while others directed traffic. Hal flicked on his lights, not needing his siren until they were away from the accident.

The Mounties were calling ahead to hold the ferry, which had just docked after a delay in crossing, so that the ambulance would get priority boarding and be the first off the boat in Farewell.

"Hold on tight," Henrik said.

Josephine smiled. "I'm used to it."

She might have been used to it, but her knuckles looked white as she gripped the handle in the side of the wall. As they cleared the road closure and moved away from the accident, the Mountie and the ambulance both flicked on their sirens. They sped across the island to the ferry. Usually a good twenty-minute drive, they were there in a flash.

Josephine closed her eyes as the ambulance rocked back and forth around the winding roads, and Henrik hoped that the baby wasn't giving her morning sickness. She kept her eyes closed, and he could tell her body was tense.

The ferry was waiting, and the ambulance was ushered onboard with the officer's cruiser. They didn't allow anyone else to board because it would take too long. Once the ambulance was secure, they closed the ferry to civilian traffic, and she slipped from her moorings, heading as fast as she could to Farewell.

Their main focus during the lightning-fast trip to St. John's was to make sure that their patient was stable. Anything could cause the injury to shift and either paralyze or kill him. Henrik had done an emergency trip like this before, but it was rare. Usually, they could get the air ambulance into Fogo.

The hospital was prepared for them as the traffic in St. John's seemed to work in their favor, and they rolled up to the trauma-bay doors with lights flashing. The trauma team was waiting as Henrik opened the doors, and Josephine helped him off-load the gurney with Hal.

"Patient was in a motor-vehicle collision. Blood pressure is seventy over sixty, and he was alert in the field. There is a broken clavicle and suspected fracture of the spine between C3 and T1. Halo was placed in the field." Josephine rattled off data as the trauma doctor took notes, not quite keeping up with how fast she was giving information.

"Are you a trauma surgeon?" the emergency doctor asked, bewildered.

"I am," Josephine stated. "And you're a resident. You'll learn, but right now we have to move."

Henrik and Hal took him into the trauma pod, where Saul was carefully taken off their gurney and placed onto a hospital one.

The doctors cleared Henrik and Hal to leave,

and Josephine signed off as the doctor who was on scene.

There was a part of her that wanted to go in after Saul. It didn't feel right to just hand him off. She should be in there, in the emergency room. It's what she was used to, and she was starting to miss the rush of the action.

They left the hospital, and Josephine kept looking over her shoulder with uncertainty as the two paramedics loaded their up gurney.

"Josephine?" Henrik asked as Hal climbed up into the ambulance.

"Huh?" she asked, distracted.

"Are you okay?"

"I am." She laughed to herself softly. "This is the first time in my career where I just handed off a patient to another trauma team. Usually, I'm the one in there dealing with the incoming patient. It felt a bit weird to be rendered useless."

"I would hardly say *useless*," Henrik said, smiling. "It was a good thing you were so close to the accident and that you were able to help and assess his injuries so quickly. Your quick thinking most likely saved his life."

"I know, it's just…different. I'm so used to the rush and the urgency of an ER. It's been an adjustment getting used to the slower-paced life of a small-town physician."

Henrik helped her up into the ambulance front

seat. "Hal, how about you rest, and I drive back to Fogo? I'm afraid we can't use the lights, and we'll have to wait for the ferry."

Hal nodded. "Fine by me."

Henrik took the driver's seat, and Hal climbed into the back to sit on the bench and secured himself in as they pulled away from the hospital to head back to Fogo. Thank goodness they weren't the only ambulance on Fogo.

It was going to take three hours to get back to the island from the main island of Newfoundland.

Josephine gazed out the window. "The fog is clearing up, and the sun is coming out. When I drove to Fogo it was raining, and I was so worried about my new job that I didn't really get to appreciate the drive."

"Well, now you can." Henrik was pleased.

The more she fell in love with Newfoundland, the more likely she would stay, and that made him happy indeed.

"Where is L'Anse aux Meadows?" Josephine suddenly asked, interrupting his thoughts.

"The Viking site?" Henrik asked.

"Yes."

"Past Farewell."

"I figured it was past Farewell, but is it far to drive in a day?"

"Yes. It's about eight hours one way, past Gros Morne National Park. Why? Do you want to go there?"

"I do. I might have to do just that on one of my weekends off. Like a mini vacation or something."

"I'll take you," Henrik offered.

"Really?" she asked, surprised. "You don't have to. I am a big girl, and I can get there myself."

"It would be my pleasure. I've been there before, and I wouldn't mind showing you around."

"I don't know if it's wise…" she whispered.

"We said platonic and professional, but how about friends? We can be that."

Josephine smiled, warmly. "Friends would be good."

"So what do you say?"

She should turn him down. She didn't want to take any more of his time, especially when this wasn't going anywhere, but truth be told it might be nice to not be alone for a while. Not that she was completely alone.

Jenn had become a good friend, but she had a kid and a husband. It would be nice to go with someone to L'Anse aux Meadows. Still, it would be a whole weekend, not just a simple day trip.

"It's a two-day trip," she pointed out.

He shrugged. "I could use a break too. Let me take you. I don't mind. I'll drive, you book the hotel rooms."

Jo did enjoy his company, and they were having

a baby together. Maybe this would be a good way for them to bond.

They could be friends. Even if they had shared that illicit kiss that neither of them had been expecting.

That kiss was anything but friendly.

And just thinking about it now made her skin heat, and she hoped she wasn't blushing too brightly, but Henrik's eyes were on the road so she was safe. At least he did mention that they should get two hotel rooms and not share, which was a slight disappointment on one hand, but a big relief on the other.

"You don't have to come," she said again.

"No. I'll take you," Henrik said, firmly. "It's a done deal. No more arguments."

"Fine. It sounds great."

And it did.

Since David had died, she'd isolated herself from a lot of people, and it was nice to have someone to spend time with. It was nice to talk to someone. She wanted Henrik to be her friend and nothing more.

Really?

Jo shook that thought away.

It didn't matter that the night after their kiss she hadn't got a wink of restful sleep, that every time she closed her eyes all she could feel was his arms around her. The way his gentle touch had made her body quiver and her heart race.

And when he kissed her, she had melted.

Just like that first time he had kissed her. Of course, a month ago she'd thought it was a harmless one-night stand. She had been so wrong about that.

It would be just easier to keep her distance from him, push him away, but she couldn't do that. For the sake of her child, their child, she had to try and make an effort to have Henrik in her life, and being friends was the easiest way.

Even though that way was risky for her heart.

They hadn't said much more on their trip back to Fogo. It was kind of hard to talk about the baby when Hal was in the back. Even though Jo was only a new Fogo Island resident, she knew very well that Hal and Lloyd were hardly discreet. If there was any mention about the baby, then the whole island—and maybe beyond—would know Doc Jo was pregnant.

And she didn't want that.

It would become apparent soon enough: by then she would be out of the dangerous first trimester and could deal with the questions.

Can you?

Henrik dropped her back off at the clinic.

She'd lost a whole day to that accident, but she didn't have many appointments that were urgent and all the urgent patients had gone to the hospital for the day.

Jenn had left her messages and a note inviting her to dinner, but Jo was too tired. She would have to make it up to Jenn and take her out to lunch at Cherry's Kitchen.

Right now, she just needed to decompress, so she headed back to her apartment to make some dinner and veg out in front of the television.

What she had to do was avoid Henrik for a couple of days to get a hold of her erratic emotions, so they could deal with this baby situation as platonically as possible.

At least she would be off emergency duty this coming week.

Which meant that she wouldn't have nearly as many run-ins with Henrik, and that was fine by her. She could get her bearings.

There was a knock at the clinic door, and she groaned inwardly. She made her way to the door and glanced out the window. It was George. She unlocked the door.

"George!" She stepped aside and let him into the clinic. "Come in."

George grinned as she shut the door behind him. "I thought I would come say goodbye. I'm flying back to Nunavut tomorrow morning."

"Thank you for all your help today."

George shrugged. "It's what I do."

"Still, you were here for training, and you didn't have to come."

"I was with Henrik when the call came in, and I didn't have anything else to do."

"Well, I'm glad we got to meet. It's not often I meet air paramedics from Nunavut."

George grinned. "I'm glad we met too. You know, Henrik is a good guy."

Josephine's heart skipped a beat. "Oh?"

"I see the way he looks at you, but he's too stubborn to tell you, and I know all about being too stubborn to see what's right in front of you sometimes."

"Well, we're friends. I'm only here for a year, and Henrik doesn't seem to want to leave Fogo. But I have to go back to Toronto."

"Okay, just thought I'd put it out there. Don't let his prickly outer shell put you off." George turned and opened the door. "I better see if I can track him down."

"He had to take the ambulance and Hal back to the hospital," Jo said.

"Have you heard the status of the tourist?" George asked.

"Not yet. I hope I do. I want Saul to make a full recovery."

George nodded. "I hope to see you again, Dr. York—Doc Jo."

He stepped out into the night and headed off toward Henrik's.

Jo locked her door and headed for bed. Henrik wasn't the only with a prickly outer shell to protect himself. She had one in her own way, and even though she liked Henrik a lot, she had to be careful of her heart.

And his.

CHAPTER EIGHT

THERE WAS A knock at his door, and Henrik went to answer it. George was standing outside.

"Finally, you're home," George exclaimed.

"Come on in," Henrik offered. "Can I get you a drink?"

"Labrador tea, if you have it," George said, following Henrik into the kitchen.

"I do," Henrik said, pulling down two mugs and a tin. "I thought you'd be back at your hotel trying to catch up on sleep."

"There's time to sleep," George remarked sitting down. "How often do I see you?"

Henrik chuckled. "Not often. When are you flying back to Nunavut?"

"Tomorrow morning, and Samantha is happy."

"How long have you two been married?" Henrik asked, flipping on the kettle.

"Seven years." George pulled out a photo. "Most recent picture of the wife and kids."

Henrik smiled. "Gorgeous. But how do you have a preteen kid?"

George chuckled. "Samantha was a widow and had a son."

"Josephine's a widow." He regretted those words the moment they slipped out of his mouth, and he cursed under his breath as the kettle whistled. He poured the tea, bringing George a mug. He didn't like talking about personal stuff with friends.

With anyone.

No one needed to know.

That was his and Josephine's business.

George was smirking. "Oh, really? Is that so?"

Henrik rolled his eyes. "Drink your tea."

"When are you going to get over whoever hurt your heart?"

"How do you know someone hurt my heart?" he asked. "I never told you that."

"You looked pretty lost when I first met you. Believe me, I know heartache and pain when I see it. I watched my sister Charlotte go through it."

Henrik sighed. "Her name was Melissa, and it was a long time ago."

"So you're over it?" George asked, but Henrik could tell George didn't quite believe him.

"I am," he replied stiffly. It was true, he was over her; what he wasn't over was the way she'd hurt him. That was something he never wanted to experience again.

"Hmm," George murmured. "It's obvious you and Jo have some kind of connection, and it's also obvious you've been together."

"How is that obvious?" Henrik asked.

"She wasn't drinking, remember? Doc Jo is so pregnant. Are you the father?"

Henrik fiddled with the handle of his mug. "Yes, but it was meant to be a one-night stand."

George laughed. "That's awesome."

"No, it's not awesome. It makes everything completely complicated," Henrik muttered.

"No, it doesn't."

"She's headed back to Toronto in a year. She's not here permanently."

"And you're trying to hatch a plan to keep her here, I bet."

Henrik frowned. "It's annoying how you can read minds."

George winked. "I'm sorry. I just know you, and I also know how it was with Samantha and me. All that denial and trying to fight our feelings."

"Josephine and I are not you and Samantha. Our situations are different."

George cocked an eyebrow. "Are they?"

Henrik stood up and took his empty mug to the sink. "Yes."

"Okay." George stood and brought his mug over. "I just want to see you happy, my friend."

"I am happy," Henrik stated.

What wasn't there to be happy about? He lived where he grew up, in a family home. He loved his work and everything to do with his life on Fogo. There was a lot to be thankful for.

Is there?

Henrik shook that niggling voice away. The one that reminded him that he didn't have family left. That he was alone.

That he was often lonely, but it was better this

way. It was better for his heart. He was tired of losing people.

Yet, the time he'd already spent with Josephine and the thought of their baby made him realize that maybe being alone wasn't all that it was cracked up to be.

But it's too risky. You'll be hurt.

And the pain of losing everyone he loved was fresh in his heart and mind again. It frightened him.

"Well, I'd better get back to the hotel." George sent a message to his cab driver. "I'm flying out early. Hopefully it won't be mauzey."

Henrik chuckled and gave him a half hug. "Or foggy."

George grinned. "It was good to see you. If you ever come back up to Nunavut for training, let me know. I'll fly you up to Cape Recluse so you can see my childhood home."

"I promise."

George shook his hand. "Take it easy, bro."

Henrik opened the door and watched as George got into his cab. He sighed and went back to the kitchen to wash the dishes.

He'd forgotten how perceptive George could be, and Henrik couldn't help but wonder if others were noticing a connection between him and Josephine. Had any of the locals guessed her condition?

He smiled, thinking about Jo and remembering the taste of her kisses and how she'd felt in his arms.

Stop thinking about her. Friends only, remember!

The best thing he could do was avoid Josephine. He was working a lot, and he knew from checking the rosters that she was no longer on emergency duty this week, which should mean fewer surprise run-ins. Except that he had promised to take her to L'Anse aux Meadows in his ploy to get her to stay. A trip to Newfoundland's most northern tip was a long way to go, but it was still worth it to convince Josephine she loved it here, which was what he wanted, wasn't it?

Still, he had to be careful. And as he flipped through his calendar, he groaned when he saw that tomorrow, bright and early, he was supposed to meet Josephine at the hospital because she was having her first ultrasound.

He rolled his eyes. Most of the staff at the hospital used discretion and wouldn't divulge personal information. As long as Lloyd or Hal didn't see him making his way to Ultrasound with Josephine.

There was a part of him that told him not to go.

To avoid the situation. Only that was cowardly, and he was anything but. This was his child, and he intended to be there.

Every step of the way, as long as Josephine let him.

Henrik was at the hospital early. Josephine had managed to get an appointment first thing for her ultrasound because she had patients to see, and he was glad of that. It meant that he got there before Hal, and he wouldn't have to take time off his shift.

Josephine was in the waiting room of Radiology when he got there.

She was calm and flipping through a magazine on crochet. Her hair was done up in a bun, and she looked put together, like she was heading to a fancy business lunch in Toronto. The only thing off was the crochet magazine. It was a quirk.

A smile tugged at the corner of his lips. "Learning about hooking?"

Her eyes widened, and then she smiled, a pink blush rising in her cheeks as she set down the magazine. "I'm never going to get used to that."

"I'm teasing."

"As a matter of fact, I am learning how to crochet. Baby Jo's mother is teaching me," Josephine said proudly. "I figure I'll crochet a baby blanket."

Henrik cocked an eyebrow. "How is that keeping a low profile if you're having a local teach you to crochet baby blankets?"

"She thinks it's for a friend," Josephine said, slyly.

"Sure." Henrik wasn't convinced as he sat down in the chair across from her and nerves had him tapping his foot. Josephine watched him.

"You nervous?" she asked.

"Well, you wanted to keep this situation quiet, until after the first trimester."

"I do, but no one is going to notice anything

here. We have an early-morning appointment, and the technician won't say anything to anyone. That breaks all kind of patient-confidentiality rules." She reached across and placed a hand on his knee. It was comforting.

"I'm sorry. I've never been in this situation. I'm not that good with babies."

"No siblings?"

He shook his head. "Nope. I'm an only child. My parents died when I was young, and my mother was my gran's only child. I've held friends' babies and helped in emergency situations involving children, but this is different."

"Yes."

"You have any nieces or nephews?" he asked.

She shook her head. "No, I don't. Only child too. And my late husband was as well. As for friends' babies…well I was always working and didn't see them or their kids much, but it'll be fine."

"Right."

"Dr. York?" a technician called out, reading her clipboard.

"Here," Josephine said, tucking her crochet magazine into her bag.

The technician smiled and then recognized Henrik. "Henrik…do you have an appointment?"

"No, Sally. I'm here with Dr. York," he said, clearing his throat.

Sally nodded. "Sure. No problem. Follow me."

Henrik followed Josephine and Sally into the ultrasound room and stood there awkwardly as Sally helped Josephine lie down.

Sally turned to Henrik, her cheeks a little red. "You might want to wait in the hall. Dr. York is not that far along, and we have to do a transvaginal ultrasound, with a probe. I'll let you know when it's okay to come back in."

Henrik nodded. "No problem."

Somewhat relieved, he stepped out into the hallway.

Jo was a doctor, and she should've remembered that a first ultrasound this early on would involve a very delicate situation that Henrik might not be comfortable with, but when she'd booked this test, she didn't know that she would be working so closely with him.

And she really didn't think when she'd invited him to come. To her, inviting him to attend was the right thing to do.

Which it was, but right now she felt kind of silly about the whole thing.

Sally made extra sure that she was draped properly before turning on the screen.

"Can I call Henrik back in now, Dr. York?" Sally asked, carefully.

"Yes. It's okay."

Sally went to the door and motioned for Henrik to join them. Henrik looked uneasy and was keeping his eyes averted, which Jo was grateful for. He took a seat on the other side of the monitor in the small, dimly lit ultrasound room.

"We won't see much, as you're only about seven weeks now," Sally said, checking the file. "But your obstetrician, Dr. Marks, wanted this dating ultrasound."

"Sounds good," Jo said, nervously.

The last time she had been on a table undergoing an ultrasound like this was when they were trying to check her ovaries for follicles, to see if she had eggs to harvest after her first round of in vitro fertilization medication.

She had been so hopeful, only to find out that there was nothing for the fertility doctors to use. Jo had been so crushed in that moment, but David had been with her there, holding her hand.

Jo swallowed the lump that formed in her throat as that memory faded from her mind. She was now feeling terrified that something happened to this baby. That the pregnancy test and the blood work she had done since then were lies.

"You won't usually be able to hear a heartbeat this early," Sally said as she brought up the image on her monitor. "But we certainly can see it!"

Jo craned her head and saw the tiny embryo. It was too early to even be considered a fetus yet, but it was there. The beating of its little heart.

She gasped, and a tear slipped from her eye. "That's it."

Sally smiled. "Yes. Looks good. It's not extrauterine, and everything is looking healthy. Dr. Marks will want another ultrasound at around sixteen weeks, but when you next see the doctor, which will be at about eleven or twelve weeks, you'll be able to hear the heartbeat on the Doppler by then."

Jo wiped tears from her eyes and then felt a warm hand slip into hers. She looked over to see Henrik smiling broadly at the screen. It made her heart skip a beat, and she squeezed his hand back, acknowledging him.

"It's wonderful," Henrik said, softly. "It's a clever-looking embryo."

She laughed. "Clever already?"

Henrik grinned. "Big and good-looking."

Sally was laughing too. "Best kind."

"Yes, b'y," Henrik agreed.

Jo chuckled. "As long as it's not too large when I go to deliver it."

"I was ten pounds," Henrik announced proudly.

Josephine groaned. "G'wan with cha."

Henrik laughed out loud. "That's not bad."

Sally finished taking her images and then printed out a picture. "Here you go. A nice first picture."

And indeed it was. Her heart was so happy she felt like she was going to burst. Henrik leaned over, and his blue eyes were sparkling, a smile on his face.

"Beautiful," he whispered.

"It is, isn't it," she said.

Henrik squeezed her shoulder. "Family."

The word caught her off guard, and she felt a little dizzy as she gazed up at him. They were a family, in a certain way.

"I'll just remove the probe, and you can leave when you're ready, Dr. York," Sally said.

Henrik turned away as the probe was withdrawn, instead of stepping out of the room. Sally cleaned up and then left.

"How are you feeling?" Jo asked.

"It wasn't what I was expecting."

"Me neither."

"I have an hour before my shift. Would you like to get a coffee?" Henrik asked. "It's a fine sunny day. We can sit outside."

"I'd like that if you can just let me get dressed first."

Henrik flushed. "Right. Sorry."

He slipped out of the room, and Jo cleaned herself up and got dressed. She headed out into the hallway where Henrik was waiting.

"Where are we getting this coffee?" she asked.

"The cafeteria. Then we can head outside."

"Lead the way."

They made their way to the hospital cafeteria and Henrik ordered himself a large black coffee with a shot of espresso and a decaf London Fog for Jo. She was craving espresso and a really strong hit of caffeine, but it wasn't good for the baby.

They made their way outside and found a bench.

They could see the village of Fogo spread out on the rocks. Fogo Island used to be separated by little towns and still had their names, but the whole island was Fogo. All the little spread-out, colorful houses made her happy.

There was a warmth to the sun, and Jo was glad about the summer weather coming. They sat side by side in silence staring out over the water, but it wasn't awkward. It was comfortable, just like it had been every time she'd been with him.

What was it about him, this man she hardly knew? She didn't know, but there was a part of her that wanted to find out.

"That was amazing," Henrik said, breaking the silence between them. "I mean, I knew you were pregnant, but it was still a sort of nebulous idea in my head, the idea of a baby."

"I know what you mean. Before my husband died, we had gone through IVF in our efforts to have a baby, but we had no luck. To be honest, when I was on that table waiting for the ultrasound, I was having a bit of anxiety about the whole thing."

"Oh?" he asked, gently. "You seemed so calm."

"I was still worried."

"You were?" he said.

Jo nodded. It was hard to talk about with him, because it was something she didn't talk about with anyone. Only David, but even then she hadn't really shared all her feelings, her worries about it.

How she'd felt like such a failure most of the time, which was silly, but that was how she'd felt.

"I was really worried that nothing was going to be there, that the baby was gone because I haven't had a lot of symptoms, like the whole puking thing."

Henrik laughed. "I'd think you'd be okay with not having that symptom."

She grinned. "It's true, but that symptom would also be a sign that it's real. That I'm really pregnant. I never thought it would happen."

Henrik reached out and gently placed his hand on her abdomen. "You are, though."

Warmth spread to her cheeks, and his simple touch meant so much to her that she placed a hand over his. Their gazes met, and she could see the tenderness in his eyes.

"George said you're a grump," Jo teased.

Henrik frowned. "What? When were you talking to George?"

"He came to say goodbye to me."

"Did he, now?" Henrik shook his head. "He's a meddler."

"A kind one."

Henrik snorted. "Yes. I suppose."

Jo glanced at her watch. "Oh, I better get back to the clinic. I have a patient in about forty minutes."

Henrik nodded, and they stood up. They walked back to the parking lot together.

"So when are we going to go sightseeing?" Henrik asked.

"You tell me when you want to go."

"I have this weekend off, which is kind of a miracle," Henrik remarked. "Would you like to go on Saturday and we can come back late Sunday night? See the Viking site early Sunday morning, since by the time we get there it'll be closed on the Saturday. Kind of a whirlwind trip, but what do you say?"

"Sure."

She still wasn't sure this was the smartest idea, but she wanted to be friends with Henrik, and he was offering.

They shared a child.

Like it or not, their lives were connected forever. And that wasn't such a bad thing, was it? She wouldn't mind being with Henrik.

The thought unsettled her.

This wasn't part of the plan, but maybe it could be. Maybe she could open her heart again, even if she was scared to.

"It's better to go before June hits and more tourists invade. It might still be somewhat quiet, and you'll be able to enjoy it."

"Maybe I'll pack a lunch."

Henrik grinned. "I'd like that. Thank you for including me in this moment."

"Of course. I'm glad you were able to come."

Henrik leaned over and kissed her cheek. "I'll message you later."

Jo watched him walk back to the ambulance bay, and she took a deep breath. She was glad that he wanted to be so involved; she only hoped that he would want to continue to be when she headed back to Toronto.

Even though she was falling in love with Fogo Island and Newfoundland, she had to go back to Ontario.

Jo sighed. Toronto was her home. Except, the more time she spent here, the more attached to it she got, and she was starting to get worried about what next year would bring, when she would have to say goodbye.

CHAPTER NINE

Jo DIDN'T SEE much of Henrik that week. He was busy working and there weren't many emergency situations where she was needed to work with him, now that she wasn't on call.

Her practice, or rather Gary's practice, was busy.

As more tourists came into town to watch the icebergs go by, a common cold seemed to rip through Nubbin's Harbor, and Josephine just hoped she didn't catch it, so she took extra vitamin C in an effort to avoid it.

She didn't want to be sick for her trip to the main island and a chance to see L'Anse aux Meadows. It would be her first real touristy thing, besides kissing a cod, that she'd done since she'd arrived in Newfoundland. And it was a place she had always wanted to see.

It might be nice to go on a mini vacation. She couldn't remember the last time she went somewhere, and it would be nice to have friendly company. Someone to chat to. She'd missed talking to someone.

You mean you miss Henrik.

It was true. She missed his company. She had gotten so used to being alone these last three years. It was easier to shut people out rather than to feel.

Especially the emptiness and loneliness that had

saturated most of her life. It was easier to ignore it by keeping people away.

Now Henrik was in her life for better or for worse.

Since he'd arrived back in the village, she had gotten used to him being around, even if they didn't get to chat much.

It was good to connect. She didn't feel so lost, so alone in the world. It was exciting to have a friend and someone to look out for her.

This week the only thing she had heard from him was a message to say they were on for Saturday and he'd pick her up at seven in the morning. Sharp.

As much as Jo wanted to sleep in, she was ready at seven and waiting outside the clinic with their picnic lunch, her small suitcase and a thermos full of coffee.

Decaf coffee.

Henrik's truck came around the corner and pulled up. Henrik got out. He was grinning, and that friendly charming smile made her heart skip a beat.

"You have a proper picnic basket and all!" Henrik remarked.

"I went to Cherry's Kitchen, and she put together a picnic for me. Something she does during tourist season."

"Smart. I didn't know she did that," Henrik remarked.

"Isn't Cherry's Kitchen your go-to place for dates?"

Henrik raised an eyebrow and saw she was smirking. "Where would you be hearing that?"

"Lloyd."

Henrik rolled his eyes. "Of course. Yes, I've taken other women there. Are you jealous?" he teased.

"Nope, I'm just surprised you didn't know about her picnic lunches." She winked, and he laughed as she folded up the blanket she'd brought.

Although, there was a bubble of jealousy at the thought of him with other women. It surprised her. She wasn't a jealous person by nature.

Don't think about it.

He was her friend and nothing more, even if secretly she would like a little bit more. Warmth crept up her neck, and she looked away, hoping he didn't notice her blush.

Again.

He took the basket and blanket and placed them in the back seat. Then he took her overnight bag and set it next to his.

"I also brought coffee. It's decaf, though," she said.

He wrinkled his nose. "Well, that's thoughtful of you."

"I need to limit my caffeine."

"I know, but decaf coffee is like drinking American beer. Weak." He chuckled at his joke.

Jo rolled her eyes. "Don't let any Americans hear that."

"An American told me that when he was up here working with the coast guard," Henrik said, winking again. "He couldn't handle the screech at all. You at least kissed the cod. He passed out with it."

Jo laughed as he opened her door and helped her up into the passenger seat. She buckled up, and Henrik climbed in and pulled away from the clinic. She opened the thermos and poured him a cup of coffee in one of the paper cups she had brought.

"Ta," he said, sipping it, making a face. "Awful. Awful."

"You suck, you know that," she said, chuckling. It was so easy to tease him, to joke with him. She liked that about him. Everyone might think he was a bit aloof or grumpy at times, and she'd heard the term *loner* tossed about by other town folk, but that wasn't the person she saw when she was with him.

When she was with Henrik, he was easy-going and friendly, like most of the residents here.

"Are you ready to see my Viking ancestors?" he asked, grinning as they made their way from Nubbin's Harbor to the ferry.

"Your Viking ancestors?" she asked.

"My dad's family is Norwegian, and my mother's family were original Newfoundlanders that descended from Irish immigrants, ages ago."

"I was wondering about your name, Henrik

Nielsen. It's a bit different from others around here."

He nodded. "My mother was a Power."

"I've heard that name."

"My gran only had my mother, but Gran had a couple of brothers, and most of their family, third cousins and the like, have moved away. Moved west."

"It seems like a lot of people move west," she remarked.

He nodded, his lips pressed together firmly. "Aye. I was engaged to a girl, and that's what she wanted too."

Jo could tell by the furrow of his brow and the stiffness of his spine it weighed heavily on him.

The jovial mood had melted away.

"Tell me about it," she said, gently.

"There's not much to tell."

Jo reached over and slipped her hand over his. He smiled sweetly, and she saw pain in his blue eyes that were usually full of mirth.

The same pain of loss she knew all too well.

"Tell me anyway."

He sighed. "We were going to get married, and I thought we were going to settle here. Make a life, like our ancestors did, but she left me the night we were going to run away together. So in a way, she left me standing at the altar, not in the literal sense. She headed out back to British Columbia. She didn't want to live with me here."

"And you didn't follow?"

His back straightened, and he frowned. "Fogo is my home. I won't leave. Other people leave, but not me. Not that I blame them. There was no work when the fisheries died down, but we're working hard to build back up, and people are gradually coming home again."

"Home is important."

"The most. So that's why it ended."

Jo wasn't sure she had a home anymore. It had been some time since she'd felt that inexplicable draw to a place where she had roots. She didn't know what else to say, so instead she tried to introduce another side of leaving home.

"Where I come from it's just too expensive. If you leave some communities in Ontario, you might not be able to buy back in, and then farmland is getting swallowed up by the urban sprawl."

Henrik shuddered. "That's terrible. The idea of urban sprawl."

She smiled. "It's a different kind of life compared to this one."

"And which one do you prefer so far?"

Jo chuckled softly to herself. "I like both."

"We'll work on that."

They pulled up to the ferry and got in the line. The ferry was off-loading the first run of passengers. It wasn't too long until they were boarding. Once Henrik's truck was secured in the hold, they got out and headed out to the passenger deck for the voyage across. As they were leaning over the rail she saw antlers in the water, which caught her off guard.

"Henrik," she exclaimed, gripping his arm. "Antlers."

He chuckled. "And there be caribou attached to those antlers."

"I still can't believe they swim across the channel. I know I've seen it before, but it's still amazing."

"Yep." Henrik nodded, like it was the most normal thing in the world to see a herd of caribou swim by, but Jo supposed, for him, it was. She watched in awe as the caribou made it to the shoreline and clambered up out of the water, shaking as they pranced away over the rock into some brush.

The ferry sounded its horn and slipped its moorings. The ferry jolted, and Henrik's arms came around her to steady her. It was comforting to have his arms around her. It felt right, and she didn't push him away. Instead she relished the feeling of being held again.

It had been a long time.

It felt wonderful.

Henrik didn't mean to reach out to wrap his arms around her, but when the ferry jerked, she fell back against his chest and so he steadied her, but Josephine didn't move away, and he didn't want to push her away.

It was lovely having her in his arms again. Her sweet scent of vanilla surrounded him, and he knew firsthand that she tasted just as sweet. It was taking all his self-control not to caress her and kiss her, like he longed to do.

Just like he'd wanted to do when he saw their baby on the ultrasound. Not that there had been much to see. It was just this little blob, but it was a little blob with a heartbeat, and it was his child. One day it would be a person, with their own personality, and he was both scared and thrilled about that.

He had been so overcome with emotion, and he saw that Josephine was holding back tears, then she'd opened her heart and told him why.

Which is why he'd finally decided to share his pain about Melissa. Even then it took him some time to tell her. He'd wanted to tell her then but hadn't been able to put it into words until just now.

Josephine understood his pain, and he understood hers.

It was easier to keep himself closed off usually. He didn't like to talk about his feelings, but she had opened up this piece of her heart to him, and he couldn't help himself from reciprocating. When he was around her, it felt right.

Henrik was still scared and fearful for his battered heart, but he wanted Josephine to stay, to be in his life, and if she left Fogo he would miss her company. So he held her close during the whole ferry ride to Farewell.

It was just an hour, such a short time, but it was worth it.

He wasn't sure that she was going to stay yet, and he wanted to savor every moment that he could with her.

The thin sliver of land of Newfoundland grew on the horizon, and he reluctantly let go of Josephine, and they headed back down to his truck to prepare to disembark. There were a couple more jolts, and the ferry moored on the other side.

Josephine settled in the passenger seat and he climbed up, waiting until the bay door opened and he could start his truck.

It was only a few minutes before the traffic from the ferry began to slowly make its way off and onto the highway. He navigated his way inland on the island to the other coast to take the highway that ran to L'Anse aux Meadows at the very tip.

"Would you like to stop for lunch at Gros Morne?" Henrik asked. They had been driving for a few hours, and it was almost noon.

"Sure. Wherever you like."

"It's a beautiful spot, but we'll have to come back another day to see it properly. Maybe take a trip up the fjords."

"Fjords?" she asked.

"I told you," he teased. "This is Viking land."

"Fitting, the inn you booked our rooms at is called the Valhalla Lodge Motel."

They approached the park gates, and Josephine

stared in wonder at the steep mountain cliffs and the water. Gros Morne Mountain loomed as they made their way into the park to find one of the many picnic sites that overlooked the ocean vista.

"You can camp here?" she asked.

"Yes, and you can hike up the mountain, but I wouldn't suggest you do that in your condition."

"No, but maybe one day," she said, offhandedly staring out the window.

His heart skipped a beat.

Maybe she was giving up on her idea of leaving, and his plan was working to get her to stay here in Newfoundland, where they could be a family.

Don't get ahead of yourself, a little voice warned.

Henrik didn't say anything as he found a fairly level picnic site with a view of the mountain and the water. Something that Josephine could manage easily. He parked the car, and they got out. She grabbed the blanket out of the back, and he took the picnic basket.

She didn't go for one of the tables but headed out into the tall grasses that were gently blowing in the sunny June wind and spread it out. It was a patchwork quilt.

"Is that one of Gary's?" Henrik asked. "I only ask because it looks like one of the ones that are done by the ladies in Nubbin's Harbor."

"Yes. It was the largest one and looked the most comfortable."

"They are comfy, and they're very warm." He

set the basket down on one corner so the blanket wouldn't blow away. Josephine sat down and began to unpack the basket. There was sparkling cider and sandwiches, both cheese and meats.

It was brilliant.

"It looks like it's turkey. I hope you like turkey." Josephine held out the sandwich.

"I do." He took it from her and unwrapped it, taking a bite of it before leaning back against the quilt.

"What's that mountain called?" Josephine asked. "The one you don't want me hiking yet."

He grinned. "Very difficult name."

"Oh?"

"Gros Morne Mountain," he said.

She smiled. "That is certainly complicated. So have you ever hiked up there?"

He nodded. "When I was doing a training session a few years back. It's steep, lots of sharp rocks and wildlife, but I think the most challenging training that I've ever done has been on northern Labrador and up into Nunavut."

"Seen a polar bear?" she asked.

He nodded. "One got a little too close to me once, but George was with me and scared it off. They're beautiful, but they are predators."

"I wouldn't mind seeing a wild one, but from a distance," she said.

"Distance is good. If you go into northern Labrador you can see them. Sometimes they wander down this way, but usually that's when they're on some sea ice."

"Poor things," Josephine remarked.

"What about me?" he asked, joking.

"Why should I feel sympathy for you?" she asked, her eyes twinkling.

"No reason. I just wanted all the attention on me." He winked and finished his sandwich, enjoying the scenery from their picnic site. It had been a long time since he'd been here for leisure. He'd seen some beautiful sites when he did travel from Fogo, but it was always for work, and he always returned to the place he called home.

"When we get to our hotel, we should stop for some great fish and chips near there. There's a little tavern near Hay Cove. If it's still there."

"I could go for some traditional fish and chips. As long as I don't have to kiss anything and it's not a sea cucumber."

Henrik cocked an eyebrow. "You're getting over your aversion to fish. Maybe you'll become a native Newfoundlander after all."

One could only hope.

They finished their lunch, packed up their garbage and headed out of the national park and back to the highway. It was still another four hours or so from Gros Morne to just outside L'Anse aux Meadows.

Josephine drifted off to sleep and slept most

of the way with her head pressed against the side of the truck as they drove to the Valhalla Lodge Motel, which was off the main highway not far from the national site. It was made of logs and really embraced the Viking flair, and there was a longhouse restaurant called Thor's Place that was attached. Since the place he wanted to take Josephine was actually closed, he thought that Thor's Place looked interesting.

Josephine checked them in. She came out of the office holding two keys. "They're adjoining, but seriously, don't be pestering me all night."

"I wouldn't do that." He grinned and took the key.

"So where is this place that you wanted to have dinner?" she asked.

"It's closed. We passed it when you were drooling on the side of my window."

Pink tinged her cheeks. "Oh, no. I wasn't snoring, was I?"

"No." He grinned. "There's a restaurant attached to the motel. How about we meet there in twenty minutes? Gives us a chance to stretch and freshen up."

"That sounds good. I'll meet you there in twenty." She picked up her overnight bag and made her way to her room. Henrik couldn't help but admire her as she walked away. He couldn't believe how much he was enjoying himself. Usually his life was mostly work, barely any play unless a tourist he fancied was in town, but he never went on trips just for pleasure like this.

Not in a long time.

Josephine seemed to drag out all the bits of him that he'd thought were locked away. There was a glimmer of light in his life again. It made him smile. He was very thankful that they had separate rooms, because he wanted to take her in his arms again and not let her go.

He wanted her to be his, and that thought scared him straight to his core.

Jo took her time freshening up. She changed out of her jeans and sweater, slipping on a sweater dress and some nice shoes. She put her hair up and changed her jewelry, then put on some more makeup. She wasn't sure how fancy Thor's Place was, but she had a feeling it wasn't a five-star wear-a-suit-or-get-out kind of place.

When she got there, Henrik was already seated. He waved and then stood up. Heat rushed to her face, realizing he had changed into different clothes too: well-fitted jeans and a fisherman's sweater that hugged his wide shoulders perfectly. It also brought out the color of his eyes and his dark hair.

He was incredibly handsome, and she could see some of the other women in the restaurant admiring him. Not that she could blame them. She had been extremely attracted to him the first time he'd spoken to her at Lloyd's bar.

Had been? That little voiced questioned her, teasing her.

Had been was not the right tense. She was still extremely attracted to him, which was part of the problem with having him in her life. Their eyes locked across the room, and a flutter in her stomach made her catch her breath.

She could get lost in those eyes. She had before.

It was so hard to remain friends with someone who you knew could make your blood sing with just a simple touch.

And right now, she wanted that touch again.

"You look beautiful," he said, as she slid into the booth opposite him. He sat down when she was settled. Their booth was tucked in the corner and overlooked the ocean.

"I love your sweater," she said, trying to be vague, but her cheeks were heating again, and she was blushing. She knew she was.

"Thanks. My gran knitted it for me a year before she died."

"She was talented," Josephine remarked.

He smiled, nodding. "Yes. She was."

The waitress came over, handing them their menus. "Can I get you something to drink, ducky?"

"Iced tea is fine," Josephine answered.

"And you, ducky?" the waitress asked, addressing Henrik.

"Brewis would be the best kind."

The waitress nodded. "Back soon, and I'll take your order."

Josephine opened the menu and saw that Thor's Place did have fish and chips but also caribou steaks.

"What're you going to have?" Henrik asked.

"I'll stick with the fish and chips. I was looking forward to it. What're you going to have?"

"Caribou," he said.

"Seriously?"

He shrugged. "I've had it before. Mind you, George's auntie cooked it up, but I'll see how this place manages it."

"Maybe I can steal a bite?" she asked, not sure if she was going to or not, but she was curious just the same.

"Perhaps," he said, slyly.

The waitress returned with their drinks and then took their orders, and it was just the two of them again. She knew that she would eventually have to bring up the subject of their baby. She knew that he wanted to be involved, but she was having a hard time picturing what that would look like in a year, when she would head back to Ontario. Yet, if she stayed she'd have to fund her own practice. Trauma surgeons weren't in high demand on Fogo.

At the very least she'd have to go to Newfoundland proper to work, and so she and the baby would still be separated from Henrik.

She flinched.

She didn't want to deprive her child of their father.

It was hard to contemplate or rationalize in her that this one-night stand, the first one she had ever had in her life, was not just for one night. He was completely part of her life from now on.

"Something seems to be gnawing at you," Henrik asked, cautiously.

"Something is." She swallowed the lump of dread that had been lodged in her throat. "You want to be involved with the baby?"

"I do. You know that I do."

"What happens after the year is up?"

Henrik frowned, only for a moment. "We'll figure it out."

"I know, being a trauma surgeon, I can usually think three steps ahead of a situation, but when I think ahead about this, I see lots of plane fares and…"

Henrik reached across the table and took her hands in his. It was reassuring and comforting. He looked into her eyes, and all that trepidation melted away.

"Josephine, I plan to be in my child's life. I promise you this. For now, let's focus on getting to know one another better, working on our friendship so we can give our baby the best possible chance of a stable childhood."

"I'd like that."

And it was true.

She wanted to be his friend. At the very least, even if her heart was telling her that she wanted more. She was just too scared to have it.

CHAPTER TEN

Jo's meal was quite good, and in the end she did try just a bite of well-done caribou meat, as anything that wasn't cooked through was a no-no. It was okay, and she would have it again if she had the chance.

After a filling dinner, they both retreated to their separate rooms as they had to get up early for when L'Anse aux Meadows opened. They were going to spend a couple hours there before heading back to Farewell in time to catch the last ferry to Fogo Island.

They checked out of their motel, Henrik grabbed coffee with a quick joke about not having to be subjected to decaf again, and they drove to the historic site as it opened for visitors.

There was a crispness in the late-spring air. The sun was rising but hadn't burned off the low-lying mists that clung to the mounds and hollows of the ancient Viking settlement hugging the coast of the ocean. Long grasses blew in the gentle breeze.

It was green, and the sky was as blue as the water. There were white caps on the waves, signaling that it was slightly windy out there.

The edge of Canada.

It certainly had that look, and she couldn't help

but wonder what the indigenous people had thought of Viking invaders.

"Amazing," Jo whispered, as they parked.

Henrik nodded. "It's indeed impressive. Let's take a walk."

They got out of his truck and paid the admission fees so they could walk around the site and the museum that housed artifacts and information about the settlement.

"People only think the Vikings traveled to Europe and Iceland, but really their migration was much farther," Henrik remarked.

"I read once that there were artifacts found in places like Northern Manitoba and Baffin Island."

Henrik nodded. "History is one of the things I like. Especially ancient history and seafaring."

She grinned. "Maybe you should dive for treasure?"

"Well, I used to want to, but honestly I have a huge respect for the ocean. My parents lost their lives to it." There was a sadness to his voice, and his gaze focused out on the blue ocean. "They went out on my dad's fishing trawler, and a storm crept up, hard and furious. They were lost."

Her heart ached for him. "How old were you?"

"Twelve."

She couldn't even begin to imagine the pain of losing her parents at that age. Instinctively she reached down to her abdomen, cradling their child.

"I'm sorry."

"I respect the ocean, and I love it, but I also hate it." His spine stiffened. "Still, it's in my blood."

"I get that. Home, where your roots are, is important."

A strange expression crossed his face. "Aye. You haven't said much about your parents. Are they still in—"

"Goderich? No, they retired to Arizona."

"Arizona? That seems random."

"They don't like the winter, and they don't like humidity, so they opted for Arizona over Florida. I really don't want to leave Canada either."

"I have no desire to leave Canada, but my unadventurous attitude has cost me much."

And she knew he was talking about his former fiancée then. "I think you're pretty adventurous."

Henrik cocked an eyebrow. "How so?"

"You say you hate the ocean and are unadventurous, yet you work with the coast guard and head up to the far north. You were out there, during that boating accident, helping to save victims. You're fixing up an old lighthouse, and you're willing to take a chance on a stranger."

Henrik grinned softly and caressed her face. "You're not a stranger anymore, Jo."

"Aren't I?" she asked, her voice catching in her throat, her body trembling in anticipation of another kiss.

"No." And he took a step closer.

Her heart was racing. She was going to say something more when there was a commotion down by the shore, and a couple of the park rangers went rushing by them.

"What's wrong?" Henrik asked, one of the rangers dashing by.

"Tourist fell into the ocean, hit their head," the ranger said.

"I'm a doctor," Jo said. "He's a paramedic. Can we help?"

The ranger looked relieved. "Yes, please follow me, but be careful the path is a bit rocky where he climbed down."

Henrik took her hand, and they followed the ranger down the path, to an out-of-bounds area where tourists weren't supposed to be.

"This has never happened. These come from aways sometimes are a bit bold," the ranger murmured.

On the beach a couple other park rangers had managed to retrieve the man from the water, and Jo could see the blood on his head. Once she had her footing, she made her way to the rangers.

"I'm Dr. York. I can help," she said. "I need you to be careful in case there's trauma to the spine."

The rangers nodded as Henrik was helping the other ranger lay out a tarp and gather supplies until the summoned paramedics could get there. The man's wife was crying.

"He was with our daughter. She's not here," the woman screamed.

"There's someone else in the water?" Henrik asked.

The hysterical woman nodded. "She's only eighteen."

Henrik was peeling off his leather jacket, his shoes, socks and jeans.

"What're you doing?" Jo asked.

"Going in after her. The water is calm here. I'll find her," Henrik stated. He pulled off his flannel shirt, holding it between his teeth as he swam out. She knew he was going use it as a sling to hold the girl.

Jo's heart was racing, worrying about him. The water was calm, but she knew there were things like undertows and sea life.

He's done this before. He said so himself.

Only, she had a hard time calming that inner dialogue. The one that kept thinking about how she'd lost David and she couldn't lose Henrik. Not when she was just getting to know him. Their baby needed him.

So do you.

Josephine shook those anxieties away, as the park rangers laid out the patient, and ignored the fact that Henrik was swimming out to find a missing girl. What she had to do was check on the girl's father. She pulled on gloves from the first-aid kit that the park rangers had.

He was bleeding badly.

Jo knelt down beside him and assessed his airway, breathing and consciousness. There was an open wound at the base of his skull and bruising under his eyes. He had hit his head hard, on what Jo could only assume was rocks.

She checked his eyes, and there was no pupillary reaction from his right eye, which meant there was trauma and bleeding in the brain.

His Glasgow Coma Scale rating was a three, at best, which was severe. He was breathing, for now.

What he needed was pressure relieved.

"Do you have a drill? For maintenance work perhaps?" Jo asked.

The park ranger who'd guided them to the shore frowned. "Yes. In the ATV. What do you need it for?"

"How long until the ambulance gets here?"

"An hour," the ranger said.

Jo worried her bottom lip. "We need to make sure his cervical spine is stabilized, and I may need that drill to make burr holes and relieve pressure or he won't make it to the hospital."

"I'll get it." The ranger disappeared and returned with the drill.

Jo pulled out the antiseptic and began to clean the drill bit and the patient's head.

There was a shout, and she turned to see Henrik carrying the girl out of the water. The other two rangers went to help him.

"How is she?" Jo called over her shoulder.

"Starting CPR," Henrik shouted back.

She turned to the ranger that was still with her, one that looked a bit nervous now. "You going to be okay to help me?"

He nodded. "I'm just doing this for the summer. I'm saving up for medical school."

"Good. As I just said, we're going to do some burr holes to relieve pressure. It'll allow the pooling blood to drain. What I need you to do is hold the head still. Think you can do that for me?"

"Yes, Dr. York. I can."

Jo was relieved as she started the drill. She could hear the ambulance coming, but this man needed the emergency field surgery if he was going to make it to the airfield to be airlifted to St. John's.

It had been some time since she'd done burr holes. Usually, in the hospital, a neurosurgeon would be on hand to do it, but at least she had done it before. She took a deep breath, made an incision and then made her first hole.

She repeated the process a couple more times. The last hole was created, and the man groaned.

Which was a good sign.

The paramedics came rushing over.

"Patient was pulled from the water. Unconscious with a Glasgow Coma Scale of three. Cranial pressure was building so I made four burr holes to relieve the pressure. If you have mannitol, I suggest dosing him with that before you airlift him to St. John's. There is an open wound to the base of the skull, so add in some antibiotics. I don't know how long he was in the water."

The paramedic nodded. "Thank you, Doctor."

Jo stepped back as the paramedics secured the patient to a backboard and inserted an IV. She cleaned off the drill and handed it back to the ranger.

"Thank you," Josephine said, "for the steady hands."

"Thank you, Dr. York," the ranger said. "We're so glad you were visiting today."

Jo turned to see Henrik wrapped in a blanket and the girl being loaded onto a gurney. She was coughing still, but she was alive. Jo made her way over to Henrik, who was shivering.

"We need to get you warm," Jo said, gently.

"I would like that."

"I think we'll reserve the rooms for another night and go back to Fogo tomorrow. I'll make the calls, and I'll drive us back."

Henrik nodded and scooped up his clothes. "I just need a couple hours to get warm."

"I think we've had enough excitement for today. We'll go back, have some warm soup for lunch and relax. Besides, the RCMP will be coming by to see us for a report, I'm sure."

She would drive to Farewell herself, but she was feeling pretty tired. This was not how she'd pictured her morning going.

Back at the motel, the only room left was the

honeymoon suite, but she didn't care. Henrik needed to have a hot shower and curl up in bed.

She could handle one night with him in the same room.

She was positive.

Henrik was still shivering. He had worn jeans and couldn't pull them back on wet, and he had lost his shirt out in the water. Like he had been taught when he'd first started learning about sea rescues, you took your shirt for a drowning victim to grasp at a bit of distance, instead of them scratching or punching you or pulling you underwater in panic.

It might seem foolish to take off clothes and run into a bitterly cold ocean, but his jeans and jacket would've weighed him down.

When they got back to the motel, he was taken aback when Jo told him there was only one room left. He would have argued, but he was just too cold, and he needed to get warm again.

He just followed her into the room and when she flicked on the lights, he rolled his eyes at the gaudy, Viking-themed honeymoon suite they had been landed with for the night. Including the heart-shaped bed and Jacuzzi in the corner.

"Oh, dear," she said, her voice laced with trepidation. "I had no idea."

"It's a warm, clean room," he said. "It's what we need."

"Right." She shut the door. "I'll go to the front

desk and ask for more blankets. You have a warm shower, and I'll be right back."

Henrik nodded as he made his way to the bathroom.

He wanted to wash the ocean off him.

More like he wanted to scrub it away. It was a battle every time, but it was one he willingly faced to save lives.

Still, washing it off him was a way to put his worries behind him for that particular day.

Rescuing someone from the ocean was common for him during tourist season and with his training. When his instinct to save lives kicked in, he could drown out that fear, the anger at the ocean for taking away his parents. He could lock away the trauma he felt and just get the job done.

A way to conquer his fear head-on.

So when he'd found that girl floating in the water, he'd done his work. Wrapped his shirt around her and brought her to shore. He'd ignored the sharp, numbing pain of the frigid water.

All that mattered was saving the life.

Adrenaline kicked in to help bring her back to shore and pump the water out of her lungs. He'd felt a smug satisfaction of winning when she'd coughed up the water and gasped for breath. After she was okay, that's when he'd realized that he had become hypothermic, and all that stuff he usually locked away came rushing back.

He wasn't even sure who'd wrapped the blanket

around him, because after the paramedics came to assist him and he had the blanket, he took a look at Jo. He saw the drill and he knew what she was doing on that beach.

And he was amazed by it all.

Amazed at her skill and ability and calm confidence.

She was beautiful, smart and kind. She was basically everything that he'd always dreamed of when it came to getting married and starting a family. It was what he thought he'd had when he was in love with Melissa, but that was a long time ago now.

He'd changed.

Have you?

Henrik turned off the shower and wrapped himself up in a towel. He crept out of the bathroom and as much as he wanted to put his clothes on, he was still shivering and suffering from some effects of hypothermia.

Clothes wouldn't help.

He clambered into the bed and pulled up the blanket. Jo entered the hotel room, and he was glad to see she had extra blankets with her.

"The soup is being brought to us," she told him.

"Great."

Jo spread out the blankets for him and leaned over. He caught the scent of her hair. She glanced at him.

"You're grinning, but your lips are still kind of blue."

"You know what the best way to heat up someone is?" He waggled his eyebrows, which made her chuckle.

"I will climb into bed with you, but I'm keeping my clothes on."

"It's a heart-shaped bed," he teased.

"It was the only room available," she said dryly as she slid in next to him, grabbing the remote from the nightstand.

"You're going to watch television?"

"Yes. I didn't bring a book, and I don't have my crochet, so we're going to veg and watch some mystery shows."

"Mystery?"

"Yes." She scrolled through the channels. "I know a certain show is on at this time—reruns—but they're fun. It's a historical detective series. He's quirky and smart."

She found the show that she wanted to watch, and he lay back as she snuggled against him. He had no real interest in the show that was on, but he was happy to be here, with her in bed with him.

"I'd heat up even faster if you were naked," he murmured, as he playfully ran his thumb in a circle on her shoulder.

Jo sat up and glared at him, with a smile tugging at the corner of her lips. "I'm not getting naked."

He chuckled. "Shame."

"If we were in the wilderness, then, yes, I would,

but we're in a warm room. You've had a hot shower and there are blankets. You'll be fine"

"I'm naked."

Jo snorted. "What?"

"I was only following basic safety protocols in situations like this."

She laughed. "It's a good thing I trust you."

It warmed his heart. "You do?"

"Of course." She smiled gently. "I can't think of why at this moment, though…"

Then she sighed, pulling off her damp jeans but leaving her oversize sweater on. He let his gaze drift over her shapely long legs, and his blood heated.

Jo snuggled up against him. "Hmm, you are still cold."

"See? I told you."

She leaned her head against his shoulder, and he drank in the scent of her, reveling in this moment of her tucked up against him. It felt right.

There was a knock at the door. She got up and hastily pulled on a pair of sweatpants before she answered it, taking the bag from a waiter who'd delivered their lunch from Thor's Place. She tipped the man and shut the door.

"Soup," she announced.

"Soup in a bag?" he teased, but he really didn't want soup. He'd rather she came back to bed instead, but this was less tempting and therefore better in the long run, he supposed.

"They're in cups with lids."

"What kind?" he asked, propping himself up on his elbow.

"Clam chowder for you. Not for me, though. I just got plain chicken noodle and some crackers." Josephine set down the bag at the little dinette table that was in the room.

"Toss me my overnight bag, and I'll get dressed," he said.

She grabbed his bag and threw it to him before turning her back to him. Henrik pulled on his clothes and made his way over to the table.

"Feeling warmer?" Jo asked.

"Much. All kidding aside, thanks for helping me back there."

"Anytime. You were amazing diving in and saving that girl." She handed him a spoon.

"You were awesome with that girl's father. Was it my eyes playing tricks, or were you actually doing brain surgery on that beach?"

"Burr holes. Hardly brain surgery."

"Burr holes is neurosurgery. That's impressive."

"It's not like I was clipping an aneurysm or something," she said.

"You took a drill and put holes in a man's head. On a beach. I think that's something worth celebrating. It probably saved his life."

Jo blushed, that pink tingeing her beautiful cheeks. "I'm sorry we're here for another night."

"I'm sorry too, but thank you again for taking care of me and getting the room sorted."

"You're welcome."

After their soup they sat back on the bed and watched television. Not saying anything. Jo curled up next to him and fell asleep on his arm so it was pinned down, but he didn't mind at all.

He should mind. This was not somewhere he thought he'd be again, feeling vulnerable and cozy with a woman, but it felt so right. It felt good and easy with Jo. And he couldn't recall feeling like this with Melissa.

Ever.

What was so different about Jo?

Whatever it was, he didn't care in this moment, but he was worried for his heart when she finally left him.

He was worried about the inevitable and how much it would sting.

CHAPTER ELEVEN

IT HAD BEEN two weeks since Henrik had taken Jo to L'Anse aux Meadows, and she hadn't seen much of him since they got back to Nubbin's Harbor. The trip back to catch the ferry had been quiet. He hadn't said much, and she hadn't known how to draw him into a conversation.

She was feeling a bit awkward about their night together.

She was worried that she'd done something or that he was bothered by the fact that she'd woken up plastered to his chest.

It was embarrassing.

She'd apologized for hogging the bed and snuggling with him all night.

If she'd been aware of it, she wouldn't have done it. She was mad at herself for letting her guard down with him and sleeping so soundly practically on top of him. Henrik was her friend, not her lover.

It wouldn't take much to make him your lover, though.

Jo ignored that voice and just tried to focus on her work, which wasn't difficult to do. Or so she thought, because as hard as she tried, all she thought about was him. Something would remind her of the way he smiled, or she could almost feel the touch of his skin.

Throughout the day she would think of funny things and couldn't wait to tell him. Except, he wasn't there to talk to.

She missed him.

When they were apart, she worried so much about her feelings for him, but when she was with him, she didn't let those little anxieties creep in.

It just felt so right.

"You seem distracted," Jennifer said, interrupting her thoughts.

"What?"

Jennifer grinned, knowingly. "I'm heading for lunch. Marge called, and she's on her way."

Jo nodded. "Oh, good."

"Want me to bring you a sandwich?" Jennifer asked.

"Sure, that would be great. Thanks, Jenn."

The receptionist waved and left.

The bell over the door chimed, and Marge came in carrying a car seat with baby Jo and looking a little bit flustered.

"Hi, Dr. York," Marge said, brightly and a bit out of breath. "Sorry I'm late. I got stopped by Lloyd, and he can chatter something fierce."

"No worries," Jo said. "What's up with Lloyd?"

"Oh. Nothing," Marge said nervously, flushing. She wasn't looking her in the eye.

"What?" Jo pressed.

"Lloyd is such a gossip," Marge stated, as she followed Jo into an exam room.

"So I've heard," Jo answered dryly, as Marge lifted baby Jo out of her carrier and handed her over. Jo cradled her little namesake happily.

"Lloyd says you and Henrik are an item!" Marge blurted out.

Jo's heart skipped a beat, and she tried to keep a straight face. "What?"

Marge chuckled. "I know. Lloyd sometimes sees things that aren't always there."

"What is he seeing?" Jo wondered out loud.

"Just that you're spending a lot of time with Henrik."

"We're friends, and we work together."

"I know that."

"So why is Lloyd speculating?" Jo asked, rocking little Jo back and forth.

"No one spends time with Henrik. He's kind of a loner... Been that way since his parents died. And then when his fiancée left him."

"Melissa?" Josephine said, cursing herself for continuing this thread of discussion.

"Yes. He was crushed when she left him. We all thought Melissa would cure his grief of losing his parents, but she only made it worse, and he retreated into himself. But it's like he's been a different person lately."

"Jenn calls him a rake," Jo murmured.

Marge chuckled. "Perhaps. I can see that."

Jo's pulse was thundering in her ears, and she was sure that she was breaking out in a sweat. She didn't want to hurt him, and she didn't want to lead him on. He didn't want to leave the island. Henrik had made that perfectly clear to her, but when Gary came back from Munich, she had to go back to Toronto. Fogo Island Hospital was much too small. They didn't have openings for a trauma surgeon, and with a baby on the way there was no time for her to set up her own practice.

Why?

Jo ignored that annoying, pushy voice in her head again.

"Well—" she cleared her throat "—we're friends."

"That's good. I'm glad Henrik has a friend, and you as well, Dr. York." Marge grinned.

"Well, let's check on this little gal, shall we?" Jo said brightly, even though her gut was churning and it felt like a big knot was trying to escape from there.

Maybe Henrik was keeping his distance because he'd heard the gossip about them too.

Jo finished her exam of baby Jo and sent Marge on her way.

As Marge was leaving, Henrik entered the clinic and Jo gripped the counter, hoping that Marge didn't say anything. His coming into the clinic was just a coincidence.

"Hey, Henrik," Marge said, walking quickly past him.

"See you, Marge." Henrik turned back to her. "Hey, Jo."

"Hey, yourself. Are you my next appointment?" she asked, fumbling to pull up her appointments on her phone.

"Yep. Need a tetanus booster." Henrik held up his hand, which was bandaged.

"What happened?" Jo asked anxiously.

"I was working on my house and caught my hand on a rusty nail."

She winced, and her stomach turned slightly, which was odd. She'd seen worse stuff working in the trauma center in Toronto. "That sounds nasty."

"It didn't feel good, let me tell you," Henrik said with a grimace.

"Well, come on in, and I'll take a look at it."

"I just need the shot," he said.

Jo crossed her arms. "I'm sure, but I'm going to examine it, nonetheless."

He followed her into an exam room. She got out the tetanus vaccine as Henrik removed the bandage.

Jo leaned over to inspect it and began to sweat, but ignored it. "You did a good job of cleaning it up."

"Well, I do have some experience with wounds." He grinned and winked.

She smiled at him and did a little more cleaning, replacing the bandage and trying to ignore the churning of her stomach.

"You have a light touch," he remarked.

Her cheeks flushed with heat. "Careful how you compliment me."

Henrik cocked an eyebrow. "What do you mean?"

"The town is talking…or rather, Lloyd is talking to everyone."

"Oh, aye?" he asked, carefully.

"He's been telling everyone we're an item, and I'm sure he's been talking about our weekend away."

She prepared the needle as Henrik rolled up the sleeve of his shirt. She wiped his arm with alcohol.

"Are you serious?" he said.

"About the needle or the gossip?" she teased.

"The gossip."

"I'm afraid so." She gave him the shot and applied pressure against his arm with the cotton ball. "Apply pressure."

Henrik took over, their fingers brushing as she removed her hand. He was frowning, and she didn't blame him. The whole thing was making her upset. All she wanted to do was lie down.

"Well, I suppose people will really start speculating about it when you begin to show, so we won't have peace for much longer," he groused.

"I'm aware," she said, dryly.

She disposed of the used needle and bandages. As she put other items away, her stomach turned again and her head felt weird. She gripped the edge of the counter as the world around her started to sway.

"Jo?"

"Hm?" she asked, but she couldn't turn around to face him. She wanted to throw up, and her head was becoming clouded. She heard him move toward her, the paper on the exam table crinkling as he got up. His hands were on her shoulder, steadying her, only it didn't seem to work as the room tilted.

A sudden wave of dizziness was overtaking her. She tried to tell him that she was going to faint but couldn't form the words. Her pulse was thundering between her ears.

"Jo?"

She let go of the counter, slipping into blackness.

Henrik called for the ambulance because after he'd caught her and safely laid her on the floor, he'd had a hard time bringing her out of her faint. It was terrifying him.

"Jo, come on," he said, loudly as he cradled her. "Come on, sweetheart."

"Where you at, b'y?" Lloyd called out.

Henrik groaned inwardly. "In the back. Jo's fainted. Is the ambulance here?"

Lloyd came rushing back with a first-aid kit and knelt down. "Aye. Hal and Johanna are unloading the gurney. Why did she faint?"

"I don't know."

Henrik didn't know for certain, and he was worried about all sorts of things at the moment. He'd dealt with others fainting, but never someone he really cared about. The impact of it hit him like a ton of bricks.

Try as he might, he was falling for Dr. Josephine York, and he was angry at himself.

And now they were the talk of Nubbin's Harbor, apparently.

Still, when she fainted and wouldn't rouse, he worried. What if something was wrong with the baby? Fate seemed determined to take away his family whenever he left his guard down.

First his parents, his grandad, Melissa and then his beloved gran. He couldn't lose the baby as well. It would be too much for one heart to bear.

Johanna and Hal came into the room. Jo was moaning, but then her eyes would roll into the back of her head, and she'd faint again. It could be anything from low blood sugar to internal bleeding.

"What happened?" Johanna asked, as she helped Hal and Henrik get the doctor onto the gurney.

"She fainted five minutes ago. She can't seem to stay conscious," Henrik stated. "She'll need fluids."

"Aye, she could be dehydrated," Lloyd speculated. "She's been sick with that stomach flu, I suspect."

Henrik shook his head. "It's not the flu."

"How can you be sure?" Lloyd asked. "It's been going around the harbor for nigh on a month now."

"I'm certain." Henrik took a deep breath. Jo would probably clobber him, but Hal and Johanna needed to know so they could inform the doctors at the hospital about her condition. And honestly, it was only a matter of time before the whole of Nubbin's Harbor knew it all anyway.

She was here for ten more months. The baby would arrive before she left, and people would put two and two together.

"She's pregnant," Henrik stated.

"And how would you be knowing that?" Lloyd asked.

"Because I'm the father."

"Lord almighty," Lloyd exclaimed. "Well, let's get her to the hospital."

"I'll follow in my truck." Henrik wanted to go with her in the ambulance, but he knew once Jo was discharged she'd need a ride home and someone to take care of her, and that person was going to be him.

Hal nodded. "We'll see you there."

Lloyd still looked shocked as he left the clinic and started dispersing the small crowd that had gathered around outside.

Henrik made sure Jo was safely loaded. Jenn the receptionist had just arrived, and he let her know what was going on so she could send all urgent patients to Joe Batt's Arm.

After everything was settled, he got into his truck.

He was driving so fast he was hoping there weren't any RCMP on the road to give him a ticket for speeding. All he could think about was getting to her and making sure she was all right.

By the time he'd parked and made his way into the hospital, he found Jo conscious in an ER bed. She still looked pale and had an intravenous. At least she was alert now.

"Henrik?" she asked, as she poked his head around the curtain.

"Hey, I got here as fast as I could," he said.

"What happened? The last thing I remember is getting your tetanus shot ready. Oh, no, I didn't faint during the vaccination, did I?"

"No. I got it, and then you fainted," Henrik said, gently.

"And you called an ambulance?" Jo asked, stunned.

"You wouldn't rally. You were unconscious for a while. I was worried."

She groaned. "Oh. Now I remember feeling off."

He pulled up a chair and sat down beside her, taking her hand in his. "What has the doctor said? Is the baby okay?"

"The baby is fine," Josephine said with a tiny smile. "They're running tests."

Relief washed through him. "I'm glad. You scared me."

"Yeah, they knew I was..." Jo's eyes widened as she realized that he'd told the paramedics. "Oh, no."

"I had to tell Hal, Johanna...and Lloyd."

She groaned again. "So I guess the cat is out of the bag for good now."

"I'm afraid so. I just wanted to make sure that you and the baby were safe."

"I get it." Jo sighed. "I don't know what happened."

"You fainted, or have you forgotten?" he teased.

"I know that. It just came out of the blue."

"Dr. York?"

Henrik turned as the emergency-room doctor, Dr. Cranbook, peeked his head around the curtain.

"Dr. Cranbook," Henrik greeted him, standing up.

"Mr. Nielsen," Dr. Cranbook said, surprised.

"He's the baby's father," Jo offered. "You can tell him anything."

Dr. Cranbook nodded. "Well, we ran your blood work, and you had a drop in blood sugar. I'm going to order a requisition to test you for a fasting glucose test tomorrow so we can test for gestational diabetes."

"Okay, but the baby is all right?" Henrik asked, needing to hear it from another doctor who was not the mother.

"Yes," Dr. Cranbook said. "The heartbeat is strong, but I would like you to rest for a couple of days, at the very least, until your results for the glucose test come in."

"I can do that," Jo said.

"I'll get to work on your discharge." Dr. Cranbook left.

Jo sighed again. "I'm going to have to make sure the doctor in Joe Batt's Arm can handle my patients. So now they'll all know."

Henrik rubbed her shoulder. "Lloyd will have already told them."

She chuckled. "So then, all of Fogo knows by now."

"Yes, b'y." Henrik grinned. "As soon as you're discharged I'll take you home and look after you. I'm off work because of my hand."

"You don't have to take—"

"I do," he said, firmly cutting her off. "I don't want you fainting and being alone. So until we're sure you're going to be okay, I'll be your roommate."

"I guess I can't really argue with that."

"No. You can't."

"I'm sorry the whole town knows this soon," Jo said. "That was not my intention."

"I know. It's fine. Let's just focus on you getting stabilized."

"Thank you," Jo said, softly.

"It's the least I could do for you since you took such good care of me when I nearly succumbed to hypothermia."

She smiled at his exaggeration. "I'm a doctor. It's my job."

"And I'm a paramedic. It's also my job."

She grinned, her eyes sparkling. "I guess we have no choice, then."

* * *

It was another hour before Jo was discharged. Henrik pulled his truck to the front entrance of the hospital, and once she was loaded in, drove her straight back to her apartment over the clinic.

"I guess I get to see your place," he said.

"You mean Gary's place." She flicked on the light, and he followed her in. There was nothing cozy about it. It was white, modern and minimalistic. The furniture was sparse and didn't look comfortable at all. It just didn't seem like Jo belonged there. When he first met her, he would've pictured her as a modernist; now, not so much.

The couch was white leather and narrow. He was already regretting his decision. That couch would be like sleeping on rocks. Actually, rocks would probably be more comfortable.

Jo curled up on the couch, tucking her feet under her and hugging a white shaggy pillow that looked like a puppet had been murdered.

"I'm going to grab my stuff. I'll be back. You okay?" he asked.

"I'm fine. Really, you don't need to stay with me."

"Are you trying to get rid of me?" he asked.

"No. I wouldn't mind the company, but this couch sucks."

He chuckled. "I'm staying."

"You don't need—"

"Yes. I do. I won't take no for answer," he said, firmly.

"Fine." She threw up her hands. "No more argument from me."

She leaned back, her face pale. Henrik's heart skipped a beat, and he sat down next to her.

"I thought you were going to get your stuff?" she asked.

"Later," he said, softly. "I think you need to go to bed."

"I'm not that tired."

Henrik shook his head. "You're going to bed."

He helped her up and led her to the large king bed that was covered with quilts and got her settled. He sat next to her.

"Is there anything I can get for you?"

"No. Maybe just keep me company for a bit."

"Of course. What should we talk about? Maybe you can tell me what Marge said about me, or Jenn for that matter!"

Her eyes widened. "Who said Marge said anything about you?"

"I figure she's the one who told you about Lloyd."

Jo laughed. "All she said was that you're a loner."

"It's easier that way."

"I understand."

"And what did Jenn say?" he asked.

Jo smiled. "She called you a rake."

He chuckled. "Hardly."

"I agree. More of a rogue than a rake."

Their gazes met, and his heart skipped a beat as he looked into her eyes. What was happening to him? His loneliness had never bothered him before, but when he'd kept his distance from her since they returned from L'Anse aux Meadows, he had missed her so much.

He was lonely.

"What do your parents think of you moving here to Newfoundland...even for just a short time?" he asked.

"They think I should move to Arizona."

Henrik smiled wryly. "I'm sure it's warmer in the winter."

"Tell me about your parents," she said, softly.

"They were wonderful, loving. We had happiness and laughter."

"I'm sorry you lost them."

"I'm sorry you lost your husband," he said quietly.

Josephine squeezed his hand. "I think I'll try to sleep."

"Okay. I'll go and get my things. You rest."

Jo nodded and rolled over. Henrik slipped out of her apartment. He knew he really shouldn't stay with her. It was too much temptation.

The trouble was, he wanted to.

The problem was, he was falling for her.

Jo still felt exhausted, but she couldn't sleep. The apartment was silent, and she could hear the waves rolling outside her open window. Usually that sound calmed her, but she was on edge because Henrik was sleeping on the couch.

She could hear him tossing and turning and she knew that couch wasn't very comfortable.

She got up and made her way into the living room.

"Jo?" Henrik asked, sitting up.

"You can't sleep on the couch," she stated.

"Neither can you, if you're thinking of switching."

She crossed her arms. "We shared a bed at that motel."

"Yes. I remember. The heart-shaped one."

Jo chuckled. "It was smaller than my bed here. I think we can share for a couple of nights."

"I would argue, but Gary's couch is ridiculously awful."

"I know." She turned back and climbed into bed.

Henrik came into the room, stepping into a pool of moonlight. He was only wearing a pair of athletic shorts, and the shadows and moonlight illuminated the broad expanse of his bare chest.

Her blood heated, and she tried not to stare at him. He pulled back the covers and slid next to her.

"This is better," he murmured, closing his eyes.

He was so warm, and she liked being snuggled up against him with his arm around her. She just wanted to be held, and it was hard to sleep knowing he was so close. So instead she watched him.

Then he opened one eye and stared at her. "You're watching me. Why?"

"I can't sleep."

Which was true. What she didn't tell him was that she couldn't sleep because she was aroused by him.

That she wanted him.

"Try," he said, closing his eyes again.

"Sorry, I'm wide awake," she said.

Henrik rolled over and propped himself up on one elbow. "Would you like a bedtime story?"

"Only if it's a spooky one," she teased.

"This isn't a glorified slumber party," he muttered.

"Oh, come on. You're telling me there are no ghost stories about Fogo, or even Newfoundland for that matter?"

He scrubbed a hand over his face. "Oh, me nerves! Ye got me drove! Fine. I can tell you about the forlorn widow who walks the beach howling."

She grinned. "That sounds creepy."

"Aye, it is."

"I'm all ears."

His eyes twinkled in the dark. "You sound way too excited for this. Somehow, I don't think it will put you to sleep."

"Just tell it," Jo said, curling up on her side, watching him in the moonlight.

"Fine. Well, there's this beautiful widow, right?"

"Right."

"And she's dead," Henrik said with emphasis.

"Okay."

"And she walks along the beach. She's howling," he whispered in her ear, sending a shiver of delight through her.

"And?"

"And what? She walks along the beach howling. Now, go to sleep."

He rolled over on his side.

"That sucked," Jo huffed.

Henrik was laughing silently. "You asked for a story. I didn't say I was any good at storytelling."

"Well, that's a disappointment. I guess I'm going to have to tell the stories to our kid."

"You're not telling our kid ghost stories at night," Henrik said, flatly.

"No, but I'm a better storyteller than you. If they asked you for a fairy tale you'd be like, *There's a giant and a knight with a sword. And they're dead. The end.*"

Henrik chuckled. "Yeah, it's probably for the best that you tell the stories."

Jo sighed. "This is not how I pictured my life."

"Well, at least you're not walking along the beach howling," he said jokingly.

She grabbed a pillow and whacked him with it before jamming it back behind her head. "You know what I mean."

"Yes, I do. This is not how I pictured my life either."

"And how did you picture it? I mean, when you were young and innocent."

Henrik sighed in the darkness. "I thought I'd be a fisherman, if I'm honest. Have a wife and kids by now."

"Why aren't you a fisherman?"

"Because of the moratorium on cod fishing."

"You could harvest sea cucumbers!"

"I suppose, but after the sea took my parents, I just… I wanted to help others. I wanted to save lives. And what about you? How did you picture your life before, when you were young and un-damaged?"

"I wanted to be a doctor for as long as I can remember. I thought by now I would have kids and own a nice house…next to my late grandparents because I loved that area of Toronto, but now…"

"Now?" he asked, gently.

She didn't know.

Jo hadn't been here long, but Fogo was starting to feel like home. The way that Goderich used to feel and the way that Toronto had never seemed to.

Henrik was starting to feel like home.

"I guess I could move out to the suburbs to raise a family now, instead of a place in the city." It wasn't a lie, but it was a deflection. She didn't want to give him false hope when she was uncertain what tomorrow would hold.

CHAPTER TWELVE

JO WAS CLEARED to go back to work when her glucose-tolerance test came back clear. She didn't have gestational diabetes, but the doctors warned her to take it easy. She'd had a simple spell of syncope. It was, hopefully, a one-off. Her obstetrician also wanted her to rest and make sure she ate regularly.

Henrik was taking the doctor's words to heart. He hadn't moved out of her place and brought her lunch almost every day. Even though it was okay for him to go back home, she was finding herself not wanting him to leave.

She liked the company.

When David had died, she didn't want anyone around. She just wanted to be alone.

She'd thought it was better.

Like she could still feel his presence if it was just her there. It was foolish to think, but it got her through some lonely moments. She'd forgotten how it was not to be alone.

She had missed companionship.

Friendship.

Before, she'd been worried about what the town thought, but now everyone knew she was expecting and Henrik was the father, so it didn't matter anymore, and it didn't seem to bother Henrik at all.

They just settled into this pattern of living together for the last few days, and it was nice. They'd get up and go to work, and at night they'd share dinner and talk about their day.

It was so comfortable and easy, and she looked forward to it every day.

The more time she spent with Henrik, the more she wanted him again.

And not just as her friend.

The more they laughed and talked, the more she remembered their night of passion. She craved his touch, his kisses, but he had made it clear he didn't want a relationship, and she wouldn't push him.

"Well, I think it's great!" Lloyd said, interrupting her out of her thoughts, and she continued checking over a bump he had gotten on the head during a boisterous shed party with some tourists.

"The bump?" Jo teased.

"You and Henrik and the baby!" Lloyd exclaimed.

"Oh, that." Jo cleaned up the wound and bandaged it.

"Melissa was never good for him. Even his gran said so. That girl wanted to explore the world, and so she did. So I'm glad he has you, especially now that she's back."

Jo's breath caught in her throat. She wasn't exactly sure that she had Henrik. "She's back?"

"Aye. To visit her grandparents. She said she's thinking of moving back. It's good when the kids of Fogo eventually find their way home."

"I'm sure it is." Jo didn't know what else to say.

She knew Henrik had loved Melissa. If she was back, Jo wouldn't get in their way. Still, that green-eyed monster of jealousy rose up in her.

Melissa had left Henrik. Why was she back to stay? Jo was worried her return would interrupt Henrik's and her happy little existence.

She grew frustrated with herself for feeling that pettiness again.

She had no right to feel this way. Henrik wasn't hers. They weren't in a relationship. There were no promises between them.

Just a baby.

And, if the situations were reversed and David somehow could come back, she'd be with him. The only difference was that David was dead and Melissa was alive. If Henrik wanted a life with Melissa, she couldn't interfere. Even though she was doing what she'd said she never would do, and that was falling for Henrik.

"There's a terrible storm coming," Lloyd said, changing the subject. "It's out of season. Be sure to have your groceries and emergency supplies tucked away."

"Thanks for the tip. You're all done, Lloyd."

"Ta." He got up. "I'm off to prepare."

"Remember to take it easy," Jo warned, but she seriously doubted he would listen to her.

Jo walked Lloyd out to lock the door, as he was the last patient.

Henrik snuck in, in his paramedic's uniform. He was frowning, and she wondered if he had seen Melissa.

"Do you have emergency supplies?" he asked.

"You're the second person to mention that," Jo said.

"Well, there's a bad storm moving up the eastern seaboard."

"I'll have to see what I have."

"I'll take you shopping. I'll be on duty when it hits," Henrik said, firmly. "Grab your purse, and we'll go stock up."

There was no point in arguing. She had sent Jenn home early because the school had called her to come get her daughter Missy ahead of the storm. Jo had never been in a storm that warranted emergency supplies. She'd never been in a hurricane or any kind of ocean-based storm. The worst had been the odd snowstorm. The best thing to do was listen to Henrik, and if he wanted to take her for supplies, she would gladly follow.

"What should I be getting?" she asked.

"Water, canned goods, storm chips."

"Storm chips?" Jo asked.

He grinned. "Just tradition, but everyone gets some chips to pass the time. I'll show you. Does Gary have candles?"

"Yes."

"Good. The power will probably go out."

Jo climbed up into his truck, and they drove off.

"Do you have supplies?" Jo asked.

"I do. Not that I will need them, being on duty. Hopefully the storm will just sideswipe us."

"Lloyd said it's not usual for this kind of storm at this time of year."

"He's right. I'm hoping for a quiet weekend."

"Oh, no. Don't say that," she said, feeling dread rise within her.

"Why?" he asked, perplexed.

"Superstition in the emergency room. It's like, as an ER doctor or nurse or other frontline worker, you never walk through the main emergency doors to start your shift. Everything will go completely wrong."

"Seriously?" Henrik asked.

"Have you never heard this?" she asked.

"No. Of course, I never did talk to the ER doctors, besides giving information about the patients. I never realized you were all so neurotic."

Jo laughed as Henrik winked. They pulled up in front of the co-op. It was busy, but not as bad as Jo thought it might be given the situation.

She grabbed a cart, and they headed inside.

"I'll get you bottled water and some batteries for your flashlight," Henrik stated.

"Okay," she agreed.

"Henrik?" a female voice behind them called out.

Jo didn't need to turn around to know it was Melissa because the look on Henrik's face said it all. His eyes were wide, and he looked like he was in shock.

Another pang of jealousy stabbed her. She turned and got her first good look at the woman who had broken Henrik's heart all those years ago.

Melissa had strawberry-blond hair and green eyes with a spattering of freckles across her nose. She was also younger than her.

She was very beautiful, and Jo could see why Henrik had been in love with her.

"Melissa, what're you doing here?" he asked.

"Thinking about moving back." Melissa's eyes darted between Jo and Henrik.

"This is Dr. Josephine York," Henrik replied, stiffly.

"It's a pleasure to meet you," Jo said. "I think I'll just go round and get the rest of my supplies. Excuse me."

She walked away from Henrik and his ex. He needed space to talk to Melissa, and she couldn't blame him.

"It's great to see you," Melissa said.

At least that's what he thought she said. He was still having a hard time believing that she was there. "It's good to see you too. It's been a while."

"It has."

He didn't know what else to say.

Truth be told, he was angry that she was back.

"You completed your training as a paramedic,

then," she said, looking appreciatively at him in his uniform.

"I did, and I'm just about to go on shift, so I'd better go."

"Henrik, can we have a coffee sometime?" Melissa asked.

"Why?" he asked stiffly.

"To catch up?" she offered.

"We'll see. I'll see you around."

Henrik stormed off and found Jo getting ready to check out. When he saw her, instantly his anger melted away, and he saw that she had chips in her cart. She looked over at him and smiled, that sweet smile he already adored.

Of course, Melissa had smiled at him sweetly too, and he'd been thoroughly duped by her back then.

Don't let Melissa ruin this for you.

"You got your storm chips?" he asked, trying to calm himself down.

"I did. You okay?" she asked with concern. "Your face is like thunder. Very cloudy, very tense."

"I do feel a bit tense, but I'm okay. I just want to get you home before this storm hits."

"Hopefully it'll blow over," Jo said.

He knew she wanted to ask him about Melissa, but he didn't want to talk about it, and he appreciated that she didn't pry. That's what he liked about Jo. She didn't push him to open up. Although, she was the one person he'd confided in the most.

Seeing Melissa had annoyed him, but it didn't hurt the way it had when she'd left or the way that he'd thought it would if she ever came back.

Right now, he was just confused. All he wanted to do was focus on work and forget that Melissa was back in Nubbin's Harbor.

He didn't want to talk to her or about her.

After Josephine paid for her supplies, he dropped her off at her apartment, carrying up her water and making sure she was settled as the dark storm clouds could be seen over the ocean.

"How long are you on duty for?" Jo asked, staring out the windows toward the sea.

"Forty-eight hours straight," Henrik said. "I have to make up for that hand injury. Just in time for the storm, apparently."

"If you need help, please come get me, or let me know where to go. I'm willing to pitch in."

"You need to rest," Henrik said, firmly.

"I'm fine. I've been resting, but if there's an emergency situation… I'm a trauma surgeon, after all. I mean, I was pregnant when I tied that man's artery in the field, and I did burr holes on a beach pregnant."

Henrik smiled. "Yes, I know. I remember."

"If I'm needed, I'm here." She took his large hand in her delicate one. Usually he liked to be touched by her, but he was still bothered by Melissa's return, so he instinctively pulled his hand away.

"I'll keep that in mind. Be safe and rest."

He left the apartment. He was confused and hurt, and he just needed the distraction of work.

Just like he had when Melissa left him all those years ago and like he suspected he'd need to do when Josephine left him too.

The storm hit within twenty-four hours. It was eerily quiet. He and Hal were parked, and he just stared in the direction of the churning ocean, not that he could see much through the rain, but he knew it was there and what it looked like.

It was a cyclone. It had been a hurricane farther south, but by the time it got here it was downgraded to a cyclone, but it was strong, nonetheless.

He hadn't seen a storm like this since his parents had died. Henrik just continued to stare out the window, with the rolling waves and the wind howling and the rain coming at him sideways.

Hal had been out getting them a coffee and jumped into the passenger seat, drenched.

"It's a doozy out there, my b'y," Hal stated, handing Henrik his coffee.

"It is indeed." Henrik gripped the coffee cup and took a sip, not really tasting it, because it wasn't just the storm that was eating away at him, and neither was it Melissa. He was mad at himself for pulling his hand away from Jo's like he had, especially when she was just offering comfort.

What was he so scared of?

She understood him like no one had ever done before.

He was just so terrified of getting hurt again because if Josephine left him too, he knew it would hurt him so much more.

It would shatter his already-badly damaged heart.

The radio crackled.

"Capsized wharf in Tilting. Mass casualties. All medical personnel able to attend are requested."

Henrik set his coffee cup down and flipped on the lights and sirens. They made their way to Tilting. Henrik had seen collapsed wharves during storms, but he had a feeling this was the hotel that was built on the wharf.

He was unfortunately right, but he was not expecting to also see homes that were being washed into the ocean by hungry, angry waves.

"My God," Hal whispered in horror.

"We need Josephine and any other person with first-aid experience," Henrik said, thinking about all the casualties.

"I'll get on the horn and call in all the volunteers I can," Hal said, texting.

All Henrik could think about as he stared at the disaster laid out before him was his parents. The storm that took away his family. He couldn't think straight for a moment.

He felt like he was going to crack.

Usually he could hold it all back, but for some reason he was feeling that bite of loss particularly keenly right now.

Perhaps it was the storm that triggered him.

The one on the outside and the one raging on the inside. A storm that wanted Jo, wanted a life with her, one that wanted to take a chance on them.

One he was trying desperately to hold in because he was terrified.

As he stared down at the destruction, he vowed that everyone would be found.

No one would not know what happened to a loved one or feel the same rage he'd felt all these years.

Jo had never been in a cyclone before. It was terrifying, but when she got the call about the wharf collapsing, she knew she had to be there. So she was downstairs and ready when Lloyd swung by to get her because all emergency personnel had been called to Tilting.

The wind was tossing her around, and her yellow rain jacket's hood was plastered to the side of her face.

Lloyd grabbed the bags of emergency supplies and fastened them into the back of his truck. They didn't say anything on the short ride to Tilting. She wasn't sure what to expect when they got there, but the first thing she saw through the rain was the flashing lights from the ambulances.

Then she saw the destruction. The crumbling rock, the shattered homes and the wild sea.

"Lord have mercy," Lloyd whispered.

"I need the bags taken to that tent. That's obviously the triage area."

Jo got out of the truck. She drowned out the howling of the wind and the cries of the injured and the scared. She had to compartmentalize all of the horror that was going on around her so she could focus on the task at hand.

She could see Henrik in the fray, tending to the wounded and helping the search-and-rescue teams pull people from the rubble.

Dr. Cranbook was there with a small team from the hospital. He took one look at her and relief washed over his face.

"Dr. York, I'm so glad you're here," he said. "I could use another good trauma surgeon."

"Glad to be here, or rather, glad to be of help."

She went straight to the first patient and got to work checking vital signs and going through her mental check list of the ABCs of trauma. Airway, breathing and consciousness.

There were fractures and lacerations, and then there were people coming in from the sea with water in their lungs.

Exposure patients.

Hypothermia.

The whole gamut.

"Jo," Henrik called, waving at her frantically.

She came over to where he was crouched protectively over a small child he had pulled out of the wreckage.

"I think he might have a collapsed lung. He has a chest-wall injury," Henrik said.

"Let me listen." Jo leaned over, and she heard the air constriction and inspected the wound.

"Well?" Henrik asked.

"We're going to have to place a drain until this boy can get to the hospital, or he won't make it there."

"I'll get what you need," he said, quickly moving to gather supplies.

Jo prepped the area, cutting away the child's shirt. She had to perform a stat tube thoracostomy on a kid. She hated doing it, but it would be the only way he'd survive the trip.

"I have a large-bore needle and an IV catheter," Henrik stated.

"I need an antibiotic," Jo said. "Is there any cefazolin?"

"Here." He handed it to her.

Jo prepped everything. She didn't have to instruct Henrik further as they worked together to get the boy ready for the chest tube. It was like he knew what she was thinking, and it made the whole procedure that much easier.

Jo took the scalpel and made a transverse incision. She inserted the clamp on the pleura, and a rush of air came out, which made her smile in satisfaction. She had found the right spot. She inserted the tube catheter and sutured it into place.

The boy started to breathe easier, and he moaned.

Henrik grinned at her. "Good job, Doc."

"Good job recognizing it. He'll need to be taken right away to the hospital."

"I'll take him." Henrik motioned to Hal, and they loaded the boy into their ambulance.

Jo made her way through the crowds. She looked back to see Henrik smiling anxiously at her, and a rush of pleasure washed through her.

She knew what he was thinking.

"I'll be careful," she shouted. "Go."

It was nice that someone cared about her again.

Henrik nodded and climbed into the back of the ambulance. She watched it leave. The wind was howling, and it was dangerous out there. She hoped Henrik would be okay too.

He'll be fine.

And that little reassuring voice calmed her. She took a deep breath and continued on with her work as the storm raged on, glad to see it was starting to die down.

Jo kept working until all the injured were dealt with. After six hours on her feet she was finally able to go home.

Dr. Cranbook dropped her off on his way through,

and she intended to head straight for her shower and then her bed. She'd worked longer shifts, but this had wiped her out completely, and as she glanced at the clock she realized that it had been thirty hours since Henrik had taken her to get groceries.

She tried to turn on a light, but it when it didn't come on, she remembered that the power went off just before she'd left and hadn't been restored yet. She had her quick shower in the light of a flashlight, then got into her comfiest lounge wear to climb into bed.

Before she could settle, there was a knock at the door.

Jo sighed and made her way there, answering it to see Henrik standing there. He had dark circles under his eyes.

"Henrik?"

"I wanted to make sure you were okay."

"I'm tired, but I'm fine." Jo stepped to the side. "Do you want to come in?"

"Yes, please." He stepped inside, and she closed the door. Instantly she noticed he looked agitated.

"Are you okay?" she asked, gently.

"No." He scrubbed a hand over his face. "A lot has been happening."

"I noticed. Do you want to sit down?"

"No." Henrik paced.

"Okay, you pace. I'll sit." She settled in her chair, watching him closely. "Is it Melissa?"

Henrik stopped. "Partly."

"I can only imagine," she said, softly.

David hadn't chosen to leave her, so her heart had been broken a different way from Henrik's. Then, the more time she'd spent with Henrik, the more she'd discovered it had healed, which made her sad because she felt like she was betraying David. Only, she knew she wasn't.

Even since she'd got pregnant, she'd been feeling this guilt and fighting feelings for Henrik. Regretful that she and David had never had this chance, yet at the same time she was so thrilled to be pregnant, to become a mother. Henrik didn't know why Melissa had left him, and a stranger was carrying his child, so it was no wonder he was struggling too.

Are you two strangers, though?

No, they weren't. They'd become friends. They'd become close.

You've become more than friends, and you know it.

She considered that carefully. David would want her to be happy. She knew that absolutely. There was no reason to feel guilty about Henrik or the baby.

"It was today, or rather when the wharf collapsed, the storm…all of it." Henrik ran his hand through his hair.

And then she knew. "It was a storm just like this that killed your parents, wasn't it?"

He nodded. "I've assisted search and rescue before, countless times and in other storms but...we didn't recover some of the people today."

"I know."

"The sea took them, and I'm so mad I can hardly speak."

She could see his heart was breaking. She got up and didn't say a word, just pulled him into an embrace, holding him as tight as she could. At first Henrik was stiff, but then his arms came around her too.

Holding her. She could feel his heartbeat against her chest, the warmth of his body, the comfort he offered her, and she melted against him.

He touched her face, his fingers brushing her skin, making her body tremble with anticipation.

"I'd very much like to kiss you," he whispered against her ear.

This time she wouldn't try to stop it. This time she wanted to feel. She wanted to heal. She wanted this moment with him.

Here and now. Try as she might to resist, she was falling for him.

"I'd very much like you to kiss me now too," she murmured, her heart racing. She'd been fighting this for so long, telling herself she didn't need this and that one night was enough. She hadn't come here for love, but it was finding her, nevertheless.

Henrik smiled, and her pulse thundered in her ears as his lips hovered over hers. Her mouth going dry, her body trembling in anticipation. Her lips remembered his kisses. Her body longed for his.

This is where she wanted to be, in his arms, melting for him.

Vulnerable to him.

She didn't want it to end.

She wanted to savor this moment, to take it with her when she had to go back to Toronto and leave him behind.

You could stay.

She flicked that thought away. Now was not the time to think. Now was the time to feel.

"Jo, I want you so much. It's hard to stop kissing you, touching you."

"So then, don't stop." She kissed him again, nibbling on his lower lip.

The kiss deepened, his tongue melding with hers. His hands ran up her back into her damp hair.

"I need you, Jo," he whispered.

All she wanted was for them to be skin to skin.

Henrik scooped her up in his arms and carried her off to bed. Her body was thrumming with excitement, longing and need. She was still a little afraid but also tired of living alone.

Like a ghost.

Tonight she could feel alive again, even if it was for a short time. Henrik set her down, brushing her cheeks.

"Don't be nervous," he said.

"I'm not."

"You're trembling."

"I know. It's because I want you, Henrik. So much."

He closed the little bit of distance between them and put his arms around her again. She could feel the hardness of his chest.

"I've tried to fight this, but I can't any longer. I've wanted you so badly too." Henrik tipped her chin and kissed her again. She swooned.

"Henrik, please."

"I know."

They moved to the bed. She wanted to feel every part of him again, to remember this moment. Her body craved it and demanded no less. She wanted to bury all the ghosts that haunted her and held her back so she could move on.

His kisses trailed from her mouth down her neck.

"You're wearing far too many clothes," he whispered, huskily, pulling her sweatshirt off.

"So are you," she teased, unbuttoning his shirt, tossing it behind her. She ran her hands over his gorgeous chest. He snatched her hand and kissed her fingertips.

"That's not where I want your kisses," she said, her voice catching in her throat.

"Oh?" he asked, smiling. He kissed lower, cupping her breasts. "And where would you like my lips, then?"

He removed her bra, and then his tongue swirled around her nipples, sending a zing of electricity through her. Henrik knelt in front of her, untying the drawstrings of her pajama bottoms and pushing them down over her hips.

Her nipples hardened as his mouth kissed her hips, the slight swell of her belly.

"Oh, God," she moaned, each press of his lips heating her blood.

Henrik picked her up and laid her down on the bed, removing his pants so she could drink in the sight of him. He leaned over her and slipped his hand under her lace underwear, stroking her and touching her.

Teasing her, making her wet and inciting her to want him all the more.

"Don't torture me," she gasped. "I want you. You know that."

He grinned, and she parted her thighs, eagerly awaiting him. He settled between them, where she could feel the hard swell of his erection at her opening, teasing her, and all she wanted was for him to be inside her.

To claim her.

To be a part of her.

She urged him to enter her, as the head of his shaft slipped into her warmth.

He moaned. "Jo… Oh, God…"

He thrust forward, filling her.

She rocked her hips, wanting him to take her harder.

Faster.

"You're so tight. You feel so good," Henrik murmured against her neck. "So good."

She ran her hands over his shoulders, holding onto him.

Not wanting to let go.

Henrik's hands skimmed her hips, controlling her movements, guiding her to an exquisite release that washed through her body like a cleansing wave. She arched her back, crying out as she came. Henrik soon followed, his thrusts coming faster and shallower until he groaned with the strength of his own release.

Henrik kissed her again tenderly and carefully withdrew.

She curled up against him, not saying anything. She just listened to the sound of his reassuring heartbeat as he held her.

It calmed her.

He was alive, and for the first time in a long time she felt alive too.

Henrik watched Jo sleep next to him, reveling in the feeling of her soft skin and the fact that she wanted to be with him in that moment when he'd been feeling so out of control and vulnerable.

He didn't like being that way in front of anyone, but he'd felt like maybe he could be with her. He couldn't recall ever feeling comfortable enough to let go with Melissa. That scarred side of him, those memories that were triggered sometimes, no one saw that side of him ever.

He'd kept it locked away, but Jo saw him.

And he saw her.

She was so beautiful.

He had been dreaming of making love to her since the first time they were together.

All during the accident, he'd struggled with emotions from the past, but then he would catch Josephine working.

He would watch her saving lives and healing.

She was an oasis of calm among the chaos and the sea.

When she was with him it felt right. He forgot about everything else.

Including his pain.

His loneliness.

This is what he wanted, even though he was still afraid to reach out and take it.

Even though it was right here in front of him.

There was a knock at the door. Jo stirred, and he rolled over, giving her a kiss on her bare shoulder.

"Stay here, I'll get it." Henrik got up and quickly dressed.

He opened the front door.

"Dr. Linwood... Gary!"

Gary looked surprised. "Henrik!"

Henrik stepped aside as Gary came in.

"I thought you were in Munich," Henrik said.

"I was, but I came back." Gary set down his bag. "Is Jo around?"

"Gary?" Jo was dressed and came out of the bedroom.

"Hi, Jo! Sorry for not calling. It was sort of a last-minute decision, and then you guys had a storm," Gary said.

"It's okay," Jo said.

"Can we talk?" Gary asked.

"Sure." Jo looked at Henrik, and he took that as his cue to leave.

"I'll head out." Henrik got his coat and left, with a knot forming in the pit of his stomach. Why was Gary back so early?

He was supposed to be gone for another ten months. That would have given Henrik time to convince Jo to stay. How would he be able to convince her now? By the looks of it, there was going to be no time left.

For one wild moment, he thought maybe that them being together last night would change her mind, but it was only for a fleeting moment.

Just because they'd made love didn't mean anything. There had been no promises between them. No declarations.

Just their baby.

He wandered around Nubbin's Harbor. The power was still out, and everything was closed. It was quiet and a good time for him to think. He made his way down to the water, picking his way over driftwood and other debris that had washed ashore.

He looked up to see an iceberg slowly making its way by.

It calmed him.

It gave him the clarity he was searching for, like it always did.

As he scanned the shoreline he caught sight of someone else walking among the rocks. It was Melissa.

For so many years he had wanted her back. He'd dreamed about Melissa returning, but then it had never happened, and he'd just grown angry.

Bitter. Cold. Hard.

He'd given up all hope.

Now here she was, and even though he didn't like that she'd hurt him, he also found he didn't really care. And with that came a sense of freedom.

Instead, he was mildly annoyed she was back and wanted to talk to him, to infiltrate his life again. She turned and looked up at him. She was smiling, but it wasn't a warm, beautiful smile like Jo had. It wasn't a smile that made his heart beat faster.

"That was some storm, eh?" she asked.

"Indeed. Is your family okay, then?"

"Yes. Grandad has a generator up and running."

"Good."

"You don't sound so okay yourself. I heard what happened in Tilting. What a tragedy," she said.

"I'm fine. Tired, but fine."

"Are you?" she asked.

"Why did you come back?" Henrik asked abruptly.

"What?" Melissa asked hesitantly.

"You didn't want to be here. You didn't want to live here."

"You're right," Melissa said. "I was young, and I didn't want to be here, but people can change."

"I didn't change," Henrik stated.

Melissa half-smiled. Like she was pitying him. "I know."

Henrik watched as she turned around and walked away. It didn't bother him watching Melissa go. What was eating away at him was that Josephine could leave soon, taking his baby with her.

Would leave.

You can still convince her to stay.

But he couldn't figure out how he was going to do that. There was nothing he could offer her. His heart was too broken. He couldn't open it up again to a killing blow, and so to protect himself he had to let Jo go.

You could go with her.

Only he couldn't do that either. It terrified him to leave. Yet it terrified him to lose Jo and the baby. He hated himself in that moment.

Hated that he was too scared to take the leap.

He loathed himself.

Fogo was in his blood. He'd promised his parents he'd wait.

It was where he was born, and it was where he'd die.

Alone.

CHAPTER THIRTEEN

Jo HAD LOTS to process. Gary didn't particularly like his work in Munich and missed Fogo. He wanted to come home. He wasn't permanently back yet. He had just flown in to talk to her face-to-face. He still had to give Munich a month's notice, and then he'd be back to take over his practice.

She had a month left on Fogo Island. That was it. In thirty days she would be returning to Toronto and to her empty house and the crowded city where she felt alone.

You don't have to.

Except that she did.

Gary was taking back his practice. It wasn't hers. There was nothing left for her here.

What about Henrik?

She had just spent a glorious night with Henrik, yes, but that wasn't a basis to stay forever. Their baby was, but she and Henrik had made no promises to each other. She knew Melissa had once meant so much to him and probably still did.

Melissa was his first love.

That she understood.

And she wasn't sure that her heart could take staying on Fogo and watching Henrik build a life with someone else.

Gary was heading to the local inn, and Jo went

for a walk. She had a lot to process. Things that she'd never thought she would have to think about when she first decided to come here, because she'd been so certain that she'd never feel that way again about someone.

Yet here she was.

She was terrified of losing her heart to Henrik when his most likely belonged to another. Her whole point of being alone these last three years was so she would never have to feel that pain of loss again.

Now, she was setting herself up for that by falling for someone who'd made it clear he didn't want a relationship with her.

Someone who had a real chance to make it work with their first love. Was she really the kind of person to stand in the way of that?

No.

She wasn't. Even if part of her wanted to.

She made her way down to the shoreline. Maybe walking by the water would give her some clarity. When she needed to clear her head she often went down to the beaches in Toronto and walked along the shore of Lake Ontario.

But at the waterfront she saw Henrik.

He was standing with his hands in his pockets, staring out over the water.

"Hey," she said, softly. "I was wondering where you went when Gary showed up."

He turned, and a shiver ran down her spine. His

expression was clouded. The walls surrounding him were up again. Just like they had been when he'd come to her place after the storm. His face softened slightly when he saw her.

"Hey, yourself. Is Gary gone now?" he asked.

"Yes. He's going to the inn. He's only here for a few days."

Relief washed over his face, and his body relaxed. "Oh, I thought he was coming back early to stay."

Jo worried her bottom lip. "He is."

"What?" Henrik exclaimed.

"He's coming back in a month. Things didn't work out in Munich. So he was super apologetic but thanked me for covering his practice."

"He can't just come back," Henrik snapped.

"Yes, he can, and he is. He owns the practice."

"Didn't you sign a contract?" he asked.

"No."

"No?" Henrik growled.

"No, because he's a friend of mine. Why are you so concerned about that?"

"I guess I'm just surprised at your irresponsibility coming all this way with no contract."

Jo crossed her arms. "I was already on a sabbatical from the hospital in Toronto. I don't actually need to work while I'm on it. Taking this position without a contract didn't hurt me in any way. I have a home, a life that's waiting for me back in Ontario."

Henrik's expression hardened. "Oh, aye, I'm sure you do."

"I do."

"So you're just going to leave?" he asked.

"Gary's coming back. Why wouldn't I go? It was never my intention to stay." She regretted the words the instant they came out of her mouth, but it was the truth. Still, the look on his face was like she had slapped him.

"I see," he said, quietly.

"My time on Fogo Island was always temporary," she said, trying to soften the truth, trying to convince herself that leaving was the right thing, even though it didn't feel like it.

"I was hoping you'd change your mind."

"Why?" she asked, hoping her voice didn't crack. Hoping he'd say he cared for her, he wanted her.

"You're carrying my child. I would like to be in its life."

"And you can't be in it if I'm in Toronto? Is that it?" she asked, trying to swallow the lump of emotion that was forming in her throat.

Henrik said nothing at first. "It's not fair."

"No. It isn't, but life isn't fair. I'm very well aware of that," she said.

"So you were just always planning to leave, then?"

"Yes. My time here was limited. I told you this."

It was the whole truth. Fogo was never permanent. No matter how much she was falling for the place. Falling for the people and the way of life.

Falling for Henrik.

"What do you have left in Toronto? What do you have in Ontario that you don't have here?"

"My home, my job…"

"Your husband's dead," he said bluntly.

That hurt.

It really stung.

She was keenly aware that David was gone and had been for some time. The house in Toronto was empty. His side of the bed was cold. He was never coming back.

"I don't understand your point," she said.

"He's not coming back. Why are you waiting for a ghost?"

"Why are you?" she asked, hotly. "Why can't you leave Fogo?"

His eyes narrowed. "I'm not waiting for anyone. Fogo is my home."

"Then, why can't you come to Ontario?"

"Fogo is my home," he repeated again, stiffly.

"What's holding you here?" she asked, turning it around on him.

"My whole life!" he replied.

"But my life…my home means nothing? I'm supposed to give it all up? For what, Henrik? What am I giving it up for?"

He didn't answer.

She knew then that this was futile. He didn't say

she was supposed to give it all up for him. He'd made it clear in the words he didn't say that he didn't want her in that way.

"I can't leave. I have to stay."

"Now who's waiting for ghosts who are never coming back? Your parents aren't coming back, are they?"

She knew his reluctance wasn't about Melissa. It was his fear about leaving. Deep down he was still that frightened boy waiting for endless, hopeless days on the beach for his parents to come home. After all this time, he was still grieving. He was still holding on to that trauma.

Aren't you holding on to yours too?

"I think we're done talking," he said, brusquely. "I have to go to St. John's."

"Why?" she asked.

"My job. The coast guard needs me. It's what I can do to help my home."

"You didn't mention this to me before. It feels like you're running away from this conversation, Henrik."

"What is there left to talk about?" he asked, loudly. "You're leaving, and I'm staying, and our baby will be schlepped between us until you decide that you don't want to do that anymore, and I'll be cut out of their life."

"I would never do that to you," she said, quietly.

He didn't seem to believe her. His face was like stone. "You say that now."

"Why do I have to be the only one to change, Henrik?"

"I never wanted to be a father like this. You didn't ask me."

"You think this is how I wanted things? We used protection. It failed. And don't pretend I'm the only one at fault here. You admitted to just being with women you thought were passing through, because you're so afraid of falling in love and having someone leave you again. Well, it takes two to tango, my friend. This is not how I wanted to be a mother either. I wanted a child with my late husband. Not some stranger in a bar!"

The tears came freely, and she was shaking. She hated saying that and instantly wanted to take it back, but she was just so angry that he was trying to lay all the blame on her.

"And that's it. The root of the problem. We are strangers." Henrik walked away then, leaving her there angry, hurt.

She watched him climb into his truck and drive away.

Stop him.

Only she couldn't move. She was so afraid. She had laid it out, asked him to give her a reason to stay, and he couldn't. When she'd come here, she hadn't wanted her heart broken again, but here she was, with her heart in pieces for the second time.

She did love him.

It terrified her how quickly she'd fallen in love with a man she barely knew.

Henrik didn't love her, though.

Not the way she loved him.

You didn't tell him you loved him either.

She was kicking herself for not telling him. It was clear to her that his reluctance to leave here had nothing to do with his ex being back and everything to do with fear, and there was nothing she could do about that until he came to that realization himself.

You could stay.

Jo wiped away the tears and made her way back to her place. Or rather, Gary's place. People were starting to wake up, ready to begin their day. There was laughter and happiness. The storm was over, and Nubbin's Harbor had weathered it. It made her love this place even more. They were tough and resilient Canadians.

Could she stay?

If she was honest, her life in Toronto was hollow and empty.

Here, her baby would have access to their father and the support of a tight-knit community.

She took a deep breath. She could call Fogo home, because this place, the people, Henrik made her feel alive again.

There was nothing left for her in Toronto. She saw that now.

Henrik might not want her, but Fogo did, and that's what she wanted again.

A place to call home.

A week later

He'd been a right arse.

As soon as the ferry docked in Farewell and he drove off, he realized what an idiot he was. If he didn't have work and a duty to the coast guard, he would've turned around and got on the next ferry back home.

Only, he was bound by duty and also realized he'd left his phone at home.

He had none of his numbers and no time to call Lloyd to track down Jo. Although, he really didn't want Lloyd knowing what an idiot he'd been.

He was positive that he'd messed everything up and she wouldn't answer even if he did manage to phone her. He knew the only way to make amends was to do it face-to-face.

So for the entire week he fretted.

Jo had been right.

All these years he wouldn't leave Fogo because he was waiting for people to return who never would. He was the one who was clinging to the ghosts of the past, not Jo.

Melissa had come back, but she wasn't the same, and he didn't even care that she was there.

What he cared about was Jo. From the first moment he'd seen her, he'd been drawn to her. Every moment with her since had felt like coming home. He was blind not to see it, to be scared to reach out for what he wanted.

To be home.

It wasn't a place. It was her. She was his home.

But he was pretty sure he'd blown his chance with her when he'd left her on that beach. When he called the clinic before he got back onto the ferry, he got the voice mail, over and over again. He was worried that she'd already left.

It didn't matter. He'd go to Toronto to find her. He couldn't let her go. He didn't want her to leave without knowing how he really felt.

He had to win her back.

No matter what it took. And he'd live wherever, just to be with her. He couldn't let Jo go.

Once he got back to Fogo he went straight to the clinic, and his heart sank when he saw a notice to say it was closed until Gary returned.

There was a sign directing people to the hospital in Joe Batt's Arm and a message that Gary would be taking over the practice again.

His heart hit the soles of his feet, and his mind raced, formulating a way to get to Toronto as fast as he possibly could.

"She's gone, my b'y," Lloyd said, walking by.

"I know."

"Dr. Linwood is coming back."

"Yes, so I've heard," Henrik said mechanically.

"I never did congratulate you on your baby with Dr. York. What a lucky twillick you'll have there, being knit by two such intelligent, well-suited people," Lloyd offered.

"Thanks," Henrik said numbly.

But Lloyd was right. He was incredibly lucky that Jo was his child's mother, and he wanted them to be a family, no matter where that was.

"I've got to run, Lloyd. I'll talk to you later," Henrik said.

Henrik needed to get to the hospital and take a vacation from his paramedic duties. He headed straight there and made his way through the ambulance bay to talk to his chief.

He glanced into the quiet emergency room and did a double take when he recognized a familiar figure going through the charts at the nurses' station.

"Jo?" he asked.

She looked up, but didn't smile the way she usually did when she looked at him. The twinkle in her eyes was gone.

And he knew it was because of him.

"Henrik! You're back."

"I am... What're you doing here?" he asked, taking a step closer to her.

"Working," she said crisply.

"I can see that, but the clinic..."

Jo crossed her arms. "What's up, Henrik?"

"I thought you'd be back in Toronto."

"I'm flying out tomorrow."

His stomach heaved.

Well, what did you expect?

"Jo…"

"Don't try to convince me to stay, because I know you don't want me—"

"I want you, Jo, and to prove it, I'll go to Toronto with you."

Her eyes widened. "I was going to say—but you cut me off—that I'm staying because this feels like home, and if you want to be with Melissa, that's okay. You love her. I get it."

"I don't love her, Jo. I love you."

Jo wasn't sure that she was hearing Henrik right, at first.

"Pardon?" she asked, finally finding her voice.

"I said, I love you." Henrik took another step closer. "And if you're going to Toronto, then so am I, if you'll have me. I want to marry you, Jo. Doesn't matter where we live. As long as we're together."

"I told you…we don't have to marry because of the baby."

"I don't want to marry you because of the baby. I want to marry you because I love you, Jo."

A lump formed in her throat. "I don't understand. A week ago you refused to leave… I put myself out there, and you didn't want me."

"I was a fool, and I was scared. Scared of losing you, and in that fear I almost pushed you away."

"You didn't push me away," she whispered.

"I didn't?" he asked.

"No, I love you too." Tears stung her eyes, and Henrik took her hands in his. "But I wasn't going to keep you from Melissa or your life here."

"The only way that you'll keep me from my life is to leave it."

Jo brushed away the tears. "I love you too. I didn't think I would ever fall in love again, but... I did. And I'm scared."

Henrik smiled and pulled her in his arms, holding her. "Me too. I've never, ever contemplated leaving home before."

"Leaving?" Josephine asked, confused.

"Toronto. Gary is coming back so..." He cocked an eyebrow. "You said you were flying out to Toronto tomorrow."

"I am. I need to sell my home. I have some logistical things to work out to make my move here permanent."

"You don't need to give up your life there," Henrik said tenderly. "I told you I'd go with you."

Jo smiled. "I know, but I already told you, this place is my home. It's where I came alive again. But I have to sell my house in Toronto so I can buy one here."

"And your practice?" Henrik asked.

"I work here now. Dr. Cranbook offered me a job when he learned Gary was returning, and I took it."

"Really?" he asked, stunned.

"Yes."

Henrik cupped her face and kissed her, making her melt. "You don't need to buy a place. Your place is with me. If you'll have me, that is."

Jo's heart felt full. Fuller than it had in years.

"Yes. I'd like that very much."

Henrik kissed her again and held her close. "I love you so much, Jo. I knew you were trouble when I spied you at the bar."

"I love you too." Jo kissed him back. "I didn't think that I would ever love again. I was wrong."

"So was I." Henrik kissed her gently, one more time. "Welcome home, Jo."

And she was home.

For the first time in years, they both were finally home.

EPILOGUE

One year later

JO WAS EXHAUSTED after her first twenty-four-hour shift since she'd returned to work after maternity leave. Not that it had been an overly eventful night, but she had learned how much she valued her sleep since having her daughter, Willa.

Willa was easy during the day and difficult at night.

She thought she'd be fine, having worked in one of the busiest emergency rooms in Toronto for many years, but there was nothing more exhausting than the earsplitting scream of a colicky baby.

Not that she would trade it for anything in the world.

Jo stifled a yawn and headed outside. Henrik was waiting for her, with a cup of coffee and a baby asleep in her car seat. One thing that always settled Willa was a nice, long car ride.

Jo gladly took the coffee from her husband.

Something she'd never thought she would ever have again. A husband. Someone to love and who loved her.

She'd come to Fogo for a change and she'd got one.

"This is great," she said, appreciatively.

"What? No *I missed you*? No throwing yourself in my arms?" Henrik teased.

Jo leaned over and kissed him. "Sorry. I did miss you."

"Good."

She peered in at the sleeping dark-haired blue-eyed little cherub she was blessed with. She was so much like her father. Henrik referred to Willa being saucy like her, and yet Jo didn't see it. She only saw Henrik's stubbornness.

"She was pretty good," Henrik said as they leaned against the side of the truck to enjoy their moment of silence and the beautiful May morning. An iceberg was meandering by out on the calm water.

"Iceberg season is beginning again," Jo said.

"Bit late this year," Henrik remarked. "It's been busy with tourists already, though. Let's just hope no storms or burr holes or…what else happened last season?"

Jo grinned. "Don't jinx yourself. Remember I'm superstitious."

Henrik chuckled softly. "Of course. How could I forget?"

Jo smiled. "Thanks for picking me up and bringing me coffee."

Henrik kissed her nose. "You know our anniversary is coming up."

"I know."

"Well, tomorrow the first part of your present is coming."

She was intrigued. "Oh?"

"Your mother."

She choked. "That's hardly romantic, but nice."

Henrik laughed. "Well, someone needs to watch Willa for the week."

"The week?" Jo asked curiously.

"We didn't go on a honeymoon, remember?"

"I can't leave on a vacation too far away from her," Jo argued. "She's still too young."

"I know. I talked to Dr. Cranbook. You're off for the week, and we're headed to L'Anse aux Meadows and the tacky, heart-shaped honeymoon suite for a couple of nights, and then a glamping experience in Gros Morne before we come back home."

Jo's heart raced. "Are you serious?"

Henrik nodded. "I am. I know it's not the most exciting trip—"

"It's perfect."

"Good. The last time we were there we couldn't do much, and this time I plan to make full use of that bed and Jacuzzi."

"Ooh, I like the sound of that." She set down her coffee cup and slipped her arms around Henrik's neck. "Have I told you lately that I love you?"

He grinned. "Yes, but I could do with hearing it again."

Josephine kissed him. "Well, I'll gladly accept your anniversary gift. What should I get you in return?"

Henrik cocked an eyebrow. "I can think of a

few things. I'm patient. I'll wait until we leave for our trip."

"Why wait? Willa is asleep, and we have that great big bed at home."

"Saucy," Henrik teased. "Well, get in so we can get home."

Jo got in the truck. Willa was still sound asleep, and she couldn't believe how lucky she was. How glad she was that she'd taken the risk and come here.

"Yes. Let's go home," she said, softly.

As she looked at her daughter and at her loving husband, she realized she really didn't need to go anywhere else.

Where they were, she'd always be home.

* * * * *

If you enjoyed this story, check out these other great reads from Amy Ruttan

A Ring for His Pregnant Midwife
Reunited with Her Surgeon Boss
Falling for His Runaway Nurse
Falling for the Billionaire Doc

All available now!